Sylvie and Star

Sylvie and Star

JULIA GREEN

OXFORD
UNIVERSITY PRESS

OXFORD
UNIVERSITY PRESS

Great Clarendon Street, Oxford OX2 6DP
Oxford University Press is a department of the University of Oxford.
It furthers the University's objective of excellence in research, scholarship,
and education by publishing worldwide in

Oxford   New York

Auckland   Cape Town   Dar es Salaam   Hong Kong   Karachi
Kuala Lumpur   Madrid   Melbourne   Mexico City   Nairobi
New Delhi   Shanghai   Taipei   Toronto

With offices in

Argentina   Austria   Brazil   Chile   Czech Republic   France   Greece
Guatemala   Hungary   Italy   Japan   Poland   Portugal   Singapore
South Korea   Switzerland   Thailand   Turkey   Ukraine   Vietnam

Oxford is a registered trade mark of Oxford University Press
in the UK and in certain other countries

British Library Cataloguing in Publication Data

Data available

ISBN: 978-0-19-275796-8

1 3 5 7 9 10 8 6 4 2

Printed in Great Britain
Paper used in the production of this book is a natural,
recyclable product made from wood grown in sustainable forests
The manufacturing process conforms to the environmental
regulations of the country of origin

For Sue,
who always wanted a dog

Chapter 1

❧

London: May

Sylvie half-walked, half-ran along the pavement on her way home from school, taking care not to step on the joins between the paving slabs. The words of a song jiggled round her head in time with her feet: *Don't step on the cracks, only on the squares, or you'll get taken by the bears . . .*

She ran past JJ's hair salon, past the Fat Friar fish and chip shop and the Express supermarket. She paused to catch her breath at the old-fashioned fruit-'n'-veg shop. Cauliflowers and aubergines, sweet potatoes, bananas, and mangos were piled outside on a table covered with pretend green-grass matting.

The nearest *real* green grass was a mile away, at the park, and it wasn't very green even there—patches of mud and yellowing grass where boys kicked footballs and teenagers swung and smoked on the swings, looking bored.

Sylvie started running again and kept going until she got to the traffic lights. She stopped to wait for the lights to change so she could cross the road. She looked up. High above the shops and office blocks that lined both sides of the street she could see a slice of pale blue sky. Sunlight glinted off the plate-glass office windows. Down here at pavement level you'd hardly know it was a sunny afternoon. Cars and lorries belched out diesel fumes. An empty plastic bag got sucked up in the after-draught of a passing bus, and whirled into the air for a few seconds, flapping like a wounded bird.

I hate it here! Sylvie thought fiercely.

But it was nearly the May holiday: just one more school day to go. And holidays meant *Italy*, and Nonna and Gramps's house in the middle of fields and woods with mountains all around and a silence so deep and beautiful that Sylvie could almost cry at the thought of it. All that, and Bella.

Bella was Nonna and Gramps's dog: a German Shepherd cross with silky fur: a mix of black and silver-grey and squirrel brown. She had brown eyes and pointed ears and the gentlest face. When Sylvie stayed at Nonna and Gramps's house, Bella hardly left her side. She padded after her round the garden. She walked with her over the fields and up through the trees in the forest . . .

The lights changed. Sylvie crossed with everyone else: a crush of people all scurrying home from shopping or school or work.

It was the thing Sylvie wanted more than anything, a dog of her own. But you can't keep a dog if you live in a flat, in a city, and your mum and dad are out at work all day. *It's not fair on the dog,* Mum said every time Sylvie asked.

It's not fair on me, either, Sylvie thought.

She turned off the main road, went down the tree-lined street with its large houses on either side. The trees had overgrown the circles of ground they'd been planted in years ago; their roots had pushed up and spread and made the tarmac buckle and crack. Poor trees! Did it hurt, pushing their roots up against the hard pavement?

Nearly there, now. She hurried down another smaller street where the houses were all joined together in terraces. Four red doors in a row, then a cut through to the estate and the blocks of flats where Sylvie lived with Mum and Dad, three staircases up.

She checked who was hanging about today. Mr Patel from the ground floor flat was putting a small bag of rubbish into one of the big green wheelie bins. He waved at her. She waved back. She pushed the heavy door to the stairwell and started to climb. Twelve steps to the first landing. Then another twelve. And twelve more. There was her blue front door. She was home.

She smelt onions and garlic the minute she opened the door. Mum must be back from work already. Good. Sometimes she was late on Thursdays—staff meetings, after-school clubs, whatever. Mum was a teacher at a comprehensive school. The same school where Sylvie would go in just over a year.

'Hi, Mum!'

'*Ciao, bambina!*' Mum's cheeks were flushed. She was stirring tomato and basil sauce at the stove. 'Good day at school? What did you do today?'

'Nothing much,' Sylvie said, the same as she always did after a school day. 'I'm just going to change.'

Taking off school uniform was like stepping out of the wrong skin and becoming *her* again. The real Sylvie. She pulled on jeans and a T-shirt. She undid her hair so it tumbled down her back, messy and comfortable. She went back into the kitchen and sat down at the table.

'There's a postcard for you,' Mum said, moving a pile of books out of the way.

Sylvie picked it up. The picture was a photo of the medieval bridge over the river Serchio. She turned it over.

> We are looking forward to seeing you!
> We will be waiting at Pisa airport.
> Bella is getting excited about all the long walks
> she'll have when you're here.
> Sunny and hot today. 30°c.
>
> Love
> Nonna and Gramps.

'You could start packing,' Mum said. 'Just a small bag this time, seeing it's only for one week. Then we can take it as hand luggage and that will speed things up at the airport.'

Something began to unwind, deep inside Sylvie. Two days to go. She went to the living room window at the front of the flat and opened it wide. The sounds of the city drifted up: traffic, sirens, the constant roar that never stopped, even at night. Far above her, a silver streak of an aeroplane climbed up into the blue sky. Hard to imagine the people inside, it looked so tiny. That would be Mum and her, in two days' time. The happy, excited feeling bubbling up inside her made her feet want to dance.

Chapter 2

❧

Italy

How was it possible? Sylvie peered out of the small aeroplane window into thin blue space. Far below, clouds made fluffy pillows. She'd flown loads and loads of times before; Mum had explained all about how planes stay up in the air (*four forces: lift, weight, thrust, and drag*) but it still felt more like magic than science.

Now they were over mountains. The clouds had cleared; she could see all the way down. It made her dizzy. The plane began the descent for Pisa airport.

'Excited?' Mum smiled at her.

Sylvie nodded. She wished Dad were here too. But he had to work this week. The bookshop opened on

Sundays, even. 'Spare a thought for the workers!' he'd said to Mum over breakfast. Sylvie knew Dad loved his job, really; he loved everything about books— reading them, talking about them, *and* selling them. He had kissed them both, and hugged Mum an extra long time, and then the taxi had arrived to take them to the airport.

The minute they were through Customs and Security, Sylvie went to buy a postcard to send to Dad straight away. That way, it might actually arrive before she got back home. She chose a second card for her best friend at school, Holly. Holly was the *only* good thing about school, Sylvie thought. She had a marmalade cat, two ginger guinea pigs, three goldfish, and a proper garden with a tree-house made by her dad. Holly had brown hair and brown eyes and olive skin, almost exactly like Sylvie. Sometimes they liked to pretend they were twins.

She queued up to pay. She'd counted out the right number of euros already. She could see Mum waiting for her at the entrance to the shop, looking out for

Nonna. And just as Sylvie got back to Mum, clutching her bag of postcards, there Nonna was: standing beneath the Arrivals Board, checking the flights.

'Nonna!' Sylvie ran up and gave her a hug. Nonna felt soft and warm and homey.

'My darling Sylvie!' Nonna hugged her back. 'You are arrived early! Let me look at you. I swear you've grown since Easter! But you are so pale! Like your mother! You poor English flowers . . .'

Mum laughed.

'Come on, let's go!' Sylvie said. 'Is Gramps waiting in the van?'

'Of course. He won't pay the airport car parking charges . . . too expensive, he says. He'll pick us up from the side road.'

It took about an hour and a half to drive to Nonna and Gramps's farmhouse. The first part of the journey was through the narrow city streets of Pisa, hemmed in by high buildings either side. The street got wider as the main road wound up a long hill. If you looked back, you had a panoramic view of the whole city basking in the sun: old houses, churches, the cathedral, and the famous leaning tower . . .

'Want to stop and look, anyone?' Gramps called out when they reached the top of the hill.

'No thanks, Dad!' Mum said.

They'd all seen the view many times before. Sylvie just wanted to get to the farmhouse. Even so, they stopped at the medieval bridge as usual at the half way point, so they could stretch their legs and use the loos and Mum and Nonna could have a cappuccino at the little café by the roadside. Gramps and Sylvie chose ice creams (chocolate and pistachio). They sat in the late afternoon sunshine to eat them. Sylvie closed her eyes, soaking it all in. Everyone was talking fast in Italian; she didn't bother to listen. Three-quarters of an hour more in the van and they'd be there.

At last they turned off the winding road, up the steep track to the farmhouse. Past the hay meadows, studded with wild flowers, past the rows of vines, up the hill towards the house. Sylvie wound her window down so she could stick her head right out and feel the sun on her face, smell the sweet scent of hot grass.

Bella was lying in the shade under the table outside on the terrace at the side of the house, but she stood up and stretched when she heard the van.

'Bella!' Sylvie called.

Bella wagged her tail. She barked and trotted towards the van.

'Stay back!' Sylvie called. She always worried that Gramps might hit the dog by mistake when he reversed the van into the parking space. But Bella kept out of the way until the van had stopped.

Sylvie opened the van door. Bella was there already, trying to squeeze herself in.

Sylvie laughed. 'Wait, you silly thing! Let me get out first! Now, come here.' She nuzzled her face in Bella's fur. Bella's tail wagged in widening circles. She whimpered and sighed, as if this was the moment she'd been waiting for too.

It was too hot to walk far in the middle of the day, even in early summer. Sylvie helped Mum and Nonna

13

carry plates and cutlery and glasses out onto the table under the shade of the vine. Nonna brought out a big bowl of salad, then a dish of lasagne: Sylvie's favourite. Bella flumped down under the table while they ate.

Sylvie's mind drifted while the adults talked on into the lazy afternoon about work, and the vegetable garden, and Uncle Vince's farm and what the grown-up cousins were up to. As soon as it got a bit cooler, she'd take Bella out for a walk.

'Do you want to leave the table?' Nonna was asking her. 'Go and unpack, Sylvie, and have a rest if you want to. Your bed's all made up ready.'

Sylvie walked round to the back of the farm-house and climbed the old wooden steps, up to the room she always slept in when she came here. It was dark: the shutters were closed to keep out the heat of the midday sun. She pushed them back, and light flooded into the room. From the window she could see all the way across the valley up to the mountains. She sat on the bed, neatly made up with white sheets and a blue blanket. Nonna had put a jug of flowers on the chest of drawers: marigolds and honeysuckle from the garden. They scented the whole room, honey-sweet. She unpacked her bag and put her clothes in neat piles in the chest of drawers. She loved doing this. Sometimes, Sylvie thought, it felt as if this was her real home, where she really belonged.

She changed out of her jeans into a cotton skirt, and put on flip-flops instead of trainers. She took the postcards and a pen out to the garden with her and lay under the cherry tree to write to Dad and Holly.

Bella wagged her tail in lazy circles. She was panting. Sylvie filled up the water bowl from the outside tap, and Bella lapped up the water in messy gulps, spilling drops onto the ground.

'Stay!' Sylvie told her when she tried to follow Sylvie when she went into the kitchen to fill a water bottle for herself. Nonna didn't allow animals inside the house. Even in winter, Bella slept outside in a wooden shed that Gramps had made especially for her. 'She's a farm dog, not a pet,' Gramps said. But he no longer had sheep or cows for Bella to round up, and vegetables and beehives, olive trees and vines didn't need a dog to look after them.

'I'm going for a walk with Bella,' Sylvie told Mum. Mum nodded. 'Just the usual places?'

'Yes.'

'Don't be longer than an hour or so,' Mum said. 'Not on our first day. Have a lovely time.'

Sylvie changed her shoes, and put the water bottle into a backpack.

'Come, Bella,' she called. They set off up the track.

Sylvie thought about what her friend Holly had said, back at school. Holly couldn't imagine being allowed to walk such long distances all by herself, in the middle of nowhere.

'It's not by myself,' Sylvie explained. 'I've always got Bella with me.'

And in any case, why not? It was just fields, and woods, trees and wild flowers, streams that dwindled to a trickle in the summer months. What harm could come to her?

'Sometimes we see deer, and goats,' Sylvie told Holly. 'There are wild boar and wolves, high in the mountains. But you hardly ever see them. They are much too shy and wild.'

Holly thought you only got wolves in stories now-adays. But Sylvie told her there were wolves in the

Italian mountains for real, lots of them. Silver-grey and reddish-gold coloured wolves, running silently along the high ridges, or slipping between the trees in the forest, moonlight dappling their fur. Sometimes in the harshest winters they came lower, to the fields to take newborn lambs, or baby goats, or chickens. That was why her uncle Vince didn't like wolves. But they never harmed humans. They would run away if they saw people.

One day, Sylvie thought, perhaps Holly could come with her to visit and she'd see it all for herself.

The track went uphill for a while; next came a fork, and if you went left you'd get to her uncle's farm, two kilometres further up the track. Today, Sylvie turned right. The track soon became a narrow path through hay meadows. The tall grass tickled her legs. She picked a bunch of wild flowers: white chicory, and blue flax. At the top of the second field, the path went along a ridge and then steep up the hillside: a stony path, easy to follow. It had been made hundreds of years ago, a mule track that joined others, linking all the small farms and hilltop villages in this part of northern Italy.

The path went deeper into the shade of beech and sweet chestnut trees. Sylvie liked knowing the names of things like the different trees and wild flowers. Mum and Gramps had taught her. Gramps knew the names of birds just by the sound of their calls. Some of the birds were the same as ones in England. Not that you saw many in London: pigeons, and ducks and seagulls in the park, and sometimes starlings, their green-black feathers peppered with white dots.

It was strangely quiet in the woods today, as if all the birds were asleep. Sunlight fell in slanting rays between the trees, making blocks of light and shadow. Where the trees were thinner and the sun got through, there were patches of grass and wild flowers. In the shadowy places, moss and ferns grew thick and bright green. It smelt sweet and earthy, as if the soil was full of leafy goodness.

Sylvie and Bella climbed on. Bella ran three times as far, going ahead and then back, checking Sylvie was following her, rounding her up. The stony path zig-zagged up the hill, higher and higher.

The trees here were spaced wider apart. Finally Sylvie and Bella emerged from the darkness of the wood into bright sunlight: a grassy hill-top with out-crops of limestone rock, white in the sunlight. Now

Sylvie could see for miles: they were on a high ridge, the edge of the mountains.

She got her bottle out of her backpack and took a long swig of water. She lay down on the dry grass. Bella flopped down too, her flanks going in and out as she panted.

Above them, the sky stretched like a blue dome. Sylvie's breath steadied; her heart settled into a calm, regular beat again. Far, far above she could see two birds of prey circle on the thermals of warm air. Higher and higher, two black dots against the blue.

She closed her eyes, perfectly happy.

Bella dozed beside her. From time to time her ears twitched: she sat up, listening intently to sounds too far off for Sylvie to hear. Her nose sniffed the air, scents that only a dog could smell. Once she whined, stood up, and the hair along her back bristled, as if she was afraid.

'What is it, Bella?' Sylvie said. She sat up, looked around. But there was nothing there. Nothing she could see, at least. 'Come on, then. Time to walk home.'

They started the walk back. It was much quicker, downhill all the way.

Chapter 3

❧

This was her life at Nonna and Gramps's house. Day after beautiful day had almost the same pattern. She woke up to sunshine. Skipped downstairs to breakfast at the big table outside. Her first job of the morning was to check for eggs: the hens were free to roam all round the garden so it took her ages, searching all the places where a new-laid egg might be hidden. She sat and watched the hens scratch the dry earth. They made gentle, crooning noises as if they were talking to each other. Sylvie loved the hens.

Bella followed her around the garden and sat down to watch too. She was used to the hens. She knew not to chase them: she'd learned when she was a puppy, seven years ago.

Next Sylvie helped Gramps or Nonna with jobs in the garden: picking spinach, watering the tomatoes, digging new potatoes, or checking the bees. At lunchtime they all ate a proper meal together, sitting round the table outside. The grown ups went on talking long after Sylvie had got down from the table.

The hottest time in the early afternoon was a quiet, lazy time, for reading or daydreaming. Nonna slept inside the house, and Gramps and Mum rested in deckchairs under the cherry trees, talking together in soft voices, or reading their books, or dozing. Later, Sylvie and Bella went for their long, hot walk up to the mountains. All the worry about school, and tests, and the bustle and noise of her ordinary city life seemed a long way away.

In the evening they ate supper together outside at the table. Nonna said home-grown, home-cooked food was the most important thing for a family: it was how she showed how much she loved them all. Eating together brought the family together. Every-one talked round the table. Sometimes Sylvie played old-fashioned board games with Nonna and Gramps before bath and bedtime. She read in bed till her eyes were droopy with sleep. *One day*, Sylvie thought, *I could live here like this all the time.*

On Thursday morning, Sylvie went downstairs as usual, to get her breakfast things from the kitchen. Nonna was making a pot of coffee, cutting bread for the toaster. It was sunny and warm already: they'd eat outside. But Bella wasn't lying under the table, and there was no sign of Mum, either.

'Has Mum gone for a walk?' Sylvie asked. 'With Bella?'

'No,' Nonna said. 'Your mother has gone on the train to Lucca, to get some shopping. Gramps drove her to the station early. She didn't think you would mind, Sylvie.'

'I don't,' Sylvie said. 'But where's Bella?'

'Down with Gramps at the vines, I expect. She doesn't go far, you know that.'

As soon as she had finished her breakfast, Sylvie went looking for Gramps. She found him in the vegetable plot, watering tomato plants. There was no sign of Bella.

'She might have gone for a little wander,' Gramps told Sylvie. 'Sometimes she follows Vince back to his place if she sees him. She'll be back.'

'Shall I help you?' Sylvie asked.

Gramps gave her the watering can. She walked between the rows of plants. Their leaves smelt herby and delicious. Some of the tomatoes were already red; Gramps picked her one to try, sweet and warm from the sun.

'I need to collect the eggs,' Sylvie said when they'd finished. 'I forgot, earlier.' She walked back up to the house, checking for Bella as she walked past the outside table, and then round to the back garden where the hens scratched and pecked or dozed in the sun. She fetched the basket from the hook on the wall and collected the eggs. Two brown speckledy ones under the nettles near the shed; a white one in a shallow scoop of warm earth shaded by leaves of spinach. She took them to the kitchen and carefully placed them in the bowl on top of the fridge.

Bella wasn't anywhere. Sylvie thought of walking to Uncle Vince's farm, to check there.

'Stop fretting,' Nonna told her. 'Come and help me make bread.'

At lunchtime, Sylvie went with Gramps to collect Mum. Her train was due in at one o'clock. They parked the van and walked through the archway of the old station house to the edge of the track. There weren't any platforms, like in England: you had to climb down steps from the train right onto the tracks.

The train came in slowly, creaking and swaying with its faded blue and white carriages. Mum stepped down looking hot and flustered, loaded with bags.

'A welcoming party!' Mum said. 'How lovely.'

Sylvie took two of the bags from Mum and carried them to the van for her. 'What did you buy?' she asked.

'Delicious ham and cheese, and some wine and lemons and groceries and some summer clothes for me. And a new magazine to read.'

'Did you bring me anything?'

Mum laughed. 'What do you think? Of course!' She fished around in one of the bags. 'Have a look in here.' She handed Sylvie a pink paper bag with something soft inside.

Sylvie slid her hand into the bag. She pulled out a skirt, in bright pink and orange cotton. Pretty. And a T-shirt with thin straps. Matching flip-flops. Italian clothes were so much nicer than ones from home.

'Do you like them? We can change them if not. I think they'll suit you.'

'Thanks, Mum. They're pretty colours.' It was funny: you could wear bright colours here in Italy where the light was so strong, but back home they didn't look right at all except on the sunniest of summer days.

'What have you been up to?' Mum asked when they got to the van.

'Sylvie's been helping Nonna and me,' Gramps said before Sylvie could get a word in. 'Hop in, you two. Belts on.' He started the engine and the van crunched across the gravel yard. They turned the corner and went up the steep slope to the main road. The pizza café was serving lunch: people sat at tables outside on the pavement. The waiter waved to Sylvie as they went past and she waved back.

'Bella's disappeared,' Sylvie said. 'She's been missing all morning.' She swallowed hard. Her throat felt tight.

Mum turned round from her seat at the front to look properly at Sylvie. 'She'll be back for her supper, you can bet on that. She's probably off visiting her doggy friends!'

Why didn't anyone take her seriously? Something was wrong. Bella had never disappeared before when Sylvie was here. She always stayed close by, padding around after her wherever she went.

Sylvie took the new clothes upstairs and put them neatly in the drawers. She closed the shutters so the room would stay cool and went back down for lunch.

Afterwards, everyone went off to rest or read or potter around. Sylvie couldn't settle to anything. She didn't feel like reading or drawing or doing anything like that. She kept wondering about Bella. What if she'd been hit by a car? Was lying injured somewhere? Or . . . Or . . .

As soon as it was cool enough, she got herself ready for a walk.

'Don't go far,' Mum said. 'Not without Bella.'

'I'm going to Uncle Vince's farm,' Sylvie said. 'To look for her there.'

'I'll come with you,' Mum said. 'I'd like to see Vince and Maria. We can have a swim, too, in their pool.'

Sylvie went back upstairs for her swimming things.

Sylvie and Mum walked slowly up the track. The fields on either side belonged to Uncle Vince. Under the trees, pale golden cows stood in groups, motionless apart from their tails flicking flies. The next field had a few sheep, and free-ranging chickens. The track ended with a gate. Mum unlatched it and they went through into the yard.

A dog barked. For a second, Sylvie thought she'd heard Bella. She ran towards the house, just as Aunty Maria stepped out into the sunshine, blinking at the brightness, her little dog at her heels.

Sylvie knelt down to stroke Tobias, her eyes filling with sudden tears. Above her head, Mum and Maria were hugging and talking fast in Italian.

'How nice of you to visit us! So hot for walking! You must have a swim straight away!' Maria said. 'Vincenzo's not here, I'm afraid. He's gone to get some part for the tractor.'

'We wondered if you'd seen Bella today?' Mum asked.

Aunty Maria shook her head. 'No. She doesn't come here much these days. Tobias is too noisy and annoying!'

Sylvie stopped stroking Tobias and stood up.

Tobias barked sharply at her.

'Shush now!' Aunty Maria told him. 'Or you will have to go back inside.'

'He wants to play,' Mum said. 'Why don't you throw his ball for him to chase, Sylvie?'

Sylvie did, for a while. Tobias fetched the ball each time and dropped it at her feet. He wagged his tail furiously and barked to make her keep throwing. Tobias was sweet enough, with his big floppy ears and tail like a flag, but he wasn't Bella.

'I'm going to swim now,' she told him. He looked at her with his brown eyes, as if he was puzzling her out. He ran back inside, tail wagging so much his whole bottom wiggled with joy.

Uncle Vince and Aunty Maria's house was like a newer version of Nonna and Gramps's. It was big and square, made of stone, with a tiled roof and wooden shutters at the windows painted green. Red and pink geranium flowers spilt over the edges of the window boxes and from earthenware pots all round the door. A big wooden table with lots of chairs stood under a shady tree in front of the house.

Sylvie walked round the side of the house to the garden behind, where the swimming pool was set in the middle of a huge grassy lawn. Uncle Vince had built it himself when his children were small. There were two of them: Sylvie's grown-up boy cousins, both away at university now.

The water gleamed, blue and inviting. Sylvie and Mum changed into swimming things while Aunty Maria went to make iced coffee. Mum settled herself into one of the sun loungers under a parasol by the pool. Sylvie climbed down the steps at the other end.

The water was cool; it felt smooth and delicious on her hot skin. She swam up and down, and then she stopped and lay back in the water, floating, eyes open, sun on her face. Swallows flew low over the pool, swooped right down to scoop beakfuls of water before darting off again over the grass. Beyond the farmhouse and the garden she could see the mountains all around, the peaks going up up into the blue sky. There were slices of white on the mountainside that from this distance looked like snow. Really, Sylvie knew, they were stone quarries where marble was cut and carried away in huge slabs on lorries. Sometimes when she was in Gramps's van they had to stop on the steep mountain road to let one of the lorries go past on a bend. Close up, there was something scary about such heavy lorries with their massive load. She imagined one tipping. Coming off the road . . .

Supposing Bella had been on the mountain road for some reason?

Her chest ached every time she thought about Bella.

Chapter 4

❦

Saturday morning, Sylvie woke up early; the sun was just coming up over the mountains. Birds were singing that fresh early morning song that usually made her happy. But the ache in her heart was there all the time now. All Thursday and Friday she'd looked and waited and still Bella hadn't come back.

Nonna, Gramps, and Mum were all worried too, now. Friday afternoon, they went looking for Bella with her: they walked up through the fields and woods, searching and calling in all the usual places where Sylvie walked with Bella. All they heard was the sound of their own voices echoing back.

Tomorrow morning, she and Mum were supposed to be flying back home. How could she leave, with Bella still missing? She would have to persuade Mum to let her stay behind . . . But Mum would say no. She'd have to run off, hide, until it was too late and the plane would have gone and everyone would be so cross with her . . .

What was that?

Sylvie sat up in bed, listening intently. The faint scritch-scratching sound came again.

Something was on the landing, just outside her door.

Her heart fluttered.

The sound came again. The clicking of claws on tiles, and a soft *whuumph*, a deep sigh.

Sylvie leapt out of bed and opened the door.

Bella was slumped on the floor outside, her fur matted and muddy, stuck with bits of leaves and grass seed. Both her ears were torn, covered in dried blood. She looked up at Sylvie, panting, and her tail feebly thumped the floor. She must have climbed all the way up the wooden steps, pushed the door open and come along the landing: all that effort to find Sylvie.

'Bella! Oh, you poor thing. Look at you. You're hurt. Where have you *been* all this time?' Sylvie hugged Bella tight.

Bella moaned, as if it hurt her to be touched. She was panting, her tongue hanging out of her sore mouth.

'Wait!' Sylvie ran along the hallway, pushed the wooden door wide open, ran down the steps to the garden to get her some water from the outside tap. Bella plodded slowly after her, as if she didn't want to be left behind. She was limping. She was thinner, too, and her eyes looked dull. Sylvie filled the water bowl for Bella three times, and still she seemed thirsty.

'Nonna?' Sylvie called out. 'Bella's come back, and she's hurt.' Her voice echoed round the quiet garden, drifted up to the shuttered windows where Nonna and Gramps slept.

No one was up yet. Mum must have heard her, though: she came hurrying out to the garden wrapping her dressing gown round her and pulling her hair back into a ponytail. Together they found antiseptic in Nonna's bathroom cupboard and poured it into a bowl of warm water so they could bathe Bella's wounds.

'Once we've cleaned her up, we'll be able to see how badly she's hurt,' Mum said.

Bella moaned, as if she was in pain. Sylvie helped hold her still, smoothing her head and whispering to her. 'Good Bella. Stay. Lie still. We're helping you. You'll be all right now.'

It didn't look quite so bad once all the blood had been wiped away.

Nonna came out of her room to make her early morning cup of tea.

'Bella's home, Nonna!' Sylvie said.

'She looks as if she's been in the wars, poor thing!' Nonna stroked Bella's head and Bella whined and tried to wag her tail. 'I'll get her something to eat.'

Gramps came to see what all the noise was about. He knelt down and felt Bella carefully all over, checked each leg and paw and felt her ribs. 'Nothing broken,' he said. He tutted at the torn ears. 'Looks like she's been in a fight with a bigger dog. Or maybe a wolf, even. She doesn't usually fight, our Bella.'

'Should we take her to the vet?' Sylvie asked.

'Later, maybe. We'll see how she gets on today. The cuts on her ears will heal, now you've cleaned them up. You've done a good job.'

Bella gulped down the food Nonna brought her. She drank more water. Then she slept. She slept almost the whole day, stretched out on the warm grass under the cherry trees.

All through that day, Sylvie kept watch over her. She brushed her matted fur as gently as she could. She pulled out the burrs and bits of forest that had got caught in the tangled fur on her belly and back. She talked to her, and smoothed her head. Bella slept on, a deep sleep.

'Look, she's dreaming!' Gramps said as he went past on his way to the kitchen in the early evening.

'If only she could talk!' Nonna said. 'I bet she'd have a story to tell us, about her adventures in the mountains.'

Bella's sides twitched and her legs kicked, as if she was running, except that she was lying on her side, still sleeping. Every so often she whimpered.

'It's all right now,' Sylvie whispered. 'You're safely home, Bella.'

'Sleep is a great healer,' Nonna said. 'She'll be much better tomorrow, you'll see.' She brought out an old blanket, and Sylvie tucked it round her to keep her warm as darkness fell. Later, Sylvie helped Mum and Gramps carry Bella into the shed, so she could sleep safe and warm all night.

Sylvie slept well too. Once, she woke up. Somewhere far off, a dog howled. Or perhaps it was a wolf, high in the moonlit mountains. Was that where Bella had been, for two whole days and nights?

And now it was Sunday. Her last morning.

Sylvie shot downstairs and out across the lawn to the shed. The grass was cool and damp on her bare feet. Bella was already awake: she yawned, got up stiffly, and stretched. She wagged her tail. She looked much better already. Sylvie buried her face in Bella's soft fur round her neck. She breathed in the doggy smell.

It was too hard, having to leave it all behind: Bella, Nonna and Gramps, the farmhouse, sunshine, the fields and mountains all around.

When she'd fed Bella and filled her bowl with water, Sylvie went back upstairs to pack her bag ready for the journey home. Next she went to collect the eggs. Bella padded slowly round after her, limping.

Seven eggs this morning. One for each of them for breakfast and three left over.

'I wish I could stay here, for ever,' Sylvie told Mum. 'You could go back without me . . . '

'How would we manage without you?' Mum said. 'Dad's missing you already, and we've only been away a week!'

Sylvie thought about Dad. She thought about Holly. Two very good reasons to go home to England. But then she thought about school, and busy streets and noise and the flat . . .

'It's only six weeks till the summer holidays, in any case,' Mum said. 'The time will flash by.'

'I'll send you progress reports,' Nonna said. 'So you know how Bella's getting on. I'll send you one of those email things if you like. Maria will help me.'

Sylvie laughed. Nonna was so old-fashioned she didn't even *own* a computer. 'Thank you, Nonna!' she said. 'I'd love that.'

'Everyone ready?' Gramps asked. 'I'll put your bags in the van.'

Sylvie gave Bella one last hug. She gave Nonna one too.

'Enjoy the journey,' Nonna said. 'Give that lovely dad of yours a big kiss from me! Tell him he should come too, next time.'

Sylvie waved from the van until she couldn't see Nonna or Bella any more.

Only six weeks, she told herself. *Six times seven days.*

Chapter 5

London: June

Sylvie skipped along the road with Dad to the bookshop on Saturday morning. It was the nicest bookshop, Sylvie thought, in the entire world. It was more like a house than a shop, with lots of small rooms. That's because it *was* an old house, the oldest building in the High Street, squeezed in between The White Horse pub and a second-hand furniture shop. It was narrow with steep steps going up three floors, and a flat at the top. The man who owned it was hardly ever there.

Dad unlocked the door and they went into the bookshop. Sylvie wished they could actually *live* here, instead of in the flat. The walls were lined with pale wooden shelves, full of new books that smelt delicious. Dad had sanded the old floorboards until they were pale golden too. It was light and airy and pretty, with big windows.

'What shall I do first?' Sylvie asked.

'Tidy the picture books in the children's corner, please,' Dad said. 'And see if you can do something about the window display in that room. It needs a freshen-up. Choose a new theme, if you like. Something summery?'

Sylvie thought about Nonna and Gramps's house in summer. The sun-baked garden. The cooler shade of the chestnut forest, and the clear blue sky above the mountains. And now, ever since Nonna's news last night . . . the bubble of excitement inside her seemed to grow bigger and bigger, so that she might burst with it!

She made herself be sensible, just for a bit longer.

Summery meant seaside to most people. Holly, for instance.

She found three picture books with sea and sand and boats on the cover. Next, she arranged the three *Ingo* books, with their beautiful underwatery covers in pink and green and blue and silver, and a series of mermaid books. She chose a non-fiction book about rock-pools and she remembered a story about seals, so she went to find that one too. She stood back to get a better look. It needed something else. Some shells, and a shrimping net, or seaweed or something else from the beach . . . she could ask Holly when she turned up.

Dad was busy sorting out new books. It was five to nine: nearly time to open up.

'Lovely!' he said, when he saw her display. 'Excellent job, Sylvie. You've earned your keep already!'

'Can I read for a bit, then?'

'Of course!'

The feeling Sylvie had, sitting cross-legged on the rug surrounded by shelves of children's books, was almost the same feeling, she thought, of being deep among the tall chestnut and beech trees in the forest near Nonna and Gramps's house. Safe, and hidden; a world within other worlds.

In the forest, she always felt as if there were a million things going on secretly, invisibly, around her: the world of bees and ants and woodlice, moths and butterflies, mice and rabbits and deer. All that shy animal and insect world was happening without her hearing or seeing any of it, most of the time.

Books were the same. It was as if behind all the bright and beautiful covers there were lives being lived; people having adventures or dreaming or thinking or talking and laughing and doing whatever was in their story. Only it was happening silently. If you opened the book, and started reading, it was as if you stepped into that world and began to hear and see it all. Your world merged into the other world.

At the till, Dad was talking to a customer about ordering a book she wanted. 'It'll be here by tomorrow,' he was saying. 'I'll give you a call to let you know it's in.'

Dad prided himself on his efficient ordering of books. 'You have to offer a service,' he sometimes said to Mum. 'That's the way we keep our customers coming in, instead of them using the internet. In the shop, we offer something special and different.'

Browsing, for example. That was what you could do in a real bookshop. You could suddenly see a book you liked the look of, and pick it up and read the cover and read inside and find it was just what you wanted to read, even though you'd never have known that before. Dad had a word for it. *Serendipity.*

Now Dad was recommending a book to someone. She heard the woman laughing. Dad was always reading books, so he could tell customers about them. All different sorts of books for different sorts of readers. The living room floor at home in their flat was piled high with books Dad was reading.

The bell on the door pinged, as someone else came into the shop.

'Good morning, Holly!' Dad said. 'Sylvie's through there.'

Sylvie stood up. Her knees felt funny from being crossed over so long. 'Hello!' she said, as Holly came into the children's section.

Holly hugged her. 'What are you reading?' Holly asked.

Sylvie showed her the book. The cover showed the head of a wolf looking one way, and a boy's head looking the other, only the boy was part of the wolf and the wolf part of the boy. Blue, against a white background.

'I've only just started it,' she said. 'The boy and the wolf know what each other are thinking. They can read their stories in their eyes.'

'Weird,' Holly said. She wrinkled her nose up. 'Are you ready?'

Sylvie nodded.

'I've got to get my mum a birthday present first.'

'You could get her a book!' Sylvie said.

Holly laughed. 'Does your dad pay you to say stuff like that?'

'No! Wish he did.'

'What book would my mum like?' Holly asked.

Sylvie thought about Holly's mum. She liked gardening, and going to the sea, and cooking, and making things for her house, and looking after old people in a care home . . . 'We'll ask Dad,' she said.

It was a short walk to Holly's house if you went across the park. Sylvie was allowed to do it as long as she was with Holly, and in the daylight. They walked across the dried-out grass under the horse chestnut trees, past the children's playground, over the football field. It was still early: there weren't many people about. Sylvie pressed her hand against her jeans' pocket and felt the folded paper, tucked safely inside. She didn't want to tell Holly yet. Not here. She was saving it up for the perfect moment.

They crossed the main road at the lights, and took the next turning down Albany Avenue to Holly's house. Holly got her key out. Her mum and dad were both out.

'What shall we do first?' Holly asked.

'Get ourselves drinks and take them up in the tree house.' Sylvie bent down to stroke Marmalade. 'You can come too,' she said to the cat. He wound himself round her legs, purring loudly.

The tree-house was the best thing about Holly's garden. Her dad had built it for Holly when she was small, and Holly and Sylvie had played princess games and pirates and the tree-house had been a castle and a ship and a lighthouse and all sorts. It was still the perfect place to sit and chat or read or have a picnic. Or tell special news.

'Look,' Sylvie said. She pulled out the folded paper from her jeans' pocket and smoothed it out. 'Read this.'

'What is it?' Holly asked.

'An email. From Nonna. I printed it out.'

Holly started to read it aloud. Sylvie knew the words off by heart already.

Sylvie darling, exciting news! We took Bella to the vet today. She is expecting puppies!!!!!!! They will be born when you are here in the summer holidays in July. So maybe that's what happened when she went missing! She was meeting her boyfriend! Making bambinos.

Holly laughed. 'Your nana says things in a funny way! What's *bambinos*?'

'Babies!' Sylvie's smile was so huge her face ached. 'Isn't it the best thing? And if Bella's having puppies then maybe at last Mum will say yes, I can have one.'

Holly looked at her. 'Are you sure? Why would she say yes now?'

'Because it's Bella! Surely?'

Holly looked doubtful. 'But you still don't have a garden . . . and your mum and dad are still at work all day.'

Sylvie's bubble of excitement deflated a bit. 'If she sees them, when they are so newborn and sweet, and realizes how good I am at looking after them . . . '

'Oh well.' Holly sounded more cheerful again. 'In any case, you can enjoy them all summer when they are tiny and cute, and that's the best bit anyway.'

'They should be born nine weeks after Bella went missing,' Sylvie said. 'I looked it all up. That's how long it takes. So that's the end of July. The twenty-ninth. Which means I'll be there, for the summer holidays. I can see the puppies being born!'

'We're going camping in Wales again for our holiday,' Holly said.

Sylvie thought about her summery window at the bookshop. She told Holly about it. 'Can I borrow a shrimping net?' she said. 'And some of your shells?'

'We need sand, too. Pebbles. Some swimming goggles or something . . . ' Holly started getting excited about all the possibilities. Holly loved a project like this. She seemed more excited about it than about the thought of puppies.

Sylvie listened as Holly talked on.

Up in the tree, hidden among the leaves, you could almost imagine you were somewhere else, not in the middle of a city at all.

Her mind started to drift. How many puppies would there be? Three? Four? What colours would they be? Would they look like Bella? Or the father dog, whoever he was? Or a bit of each. Half German Shepherd, half sheepdog? Or half Labrador? Or what?

She could hardly wait!

Chapter 6

Italy: July

Sylvie lay on the grass, watching the pattern of light and shade under the cherry tree in Nonna and Gramps's garden. A little way off, Bella slept on her side. Every so often she gave a big sigh, as if she was too hot, or fed up with waiting.

'You can't really tell she's so close to having the puppies,' Sylvie said.

'If you watch carefully, sometimes you can see them move: like a ripple along her belly,' Nonna said.

Mum laughed. 'Do you remember all of us looking at my belly, when I was expecting Sylvie?'

'You were huge! And we could see a little elbow, or a foot, as she moved about in there. Incredible.'

Sylvie squirmed. It made her feel funny, thinking about herself as a baby *inside* Mum like that. She rolled over closer to Bella, and rested her hand lightly on her belly.

'Are you too hot, too?' she said.

Bella kept her eyes closed. She made her *whuumph* sound and moved herself away from Sylvie's touch.

'Bring her water bowl over,' Mum said. 'She's too hot and tired to move.'

Sylvie walked slowly across the grass to the outside tap, filled the bowl until it flowed over and splashed her feet. The water felt deliciously cold. She carried the bowl carefully back.

Bella lapped messily at the water, and flumped back onto her side again. She closed her eyes.

The first week of the holiday it had been more like England than Italy: rain, and grey skies, and cold enough one evening for Gramps to light a fire in the wood-burning stove in the sitting room. Yesterday the weather had suddenly changed, and at last it felt like a proper Italian summer again.

Today was even hotter. Blue skies, swallows;

the sleepy heat of early afternoon. Nonna and Mum chatted and dozed in their deckchairs under the trees. Even the chickens slept in dusty nests they'd scraped for themselves in the shade of the shed.

'We should all go for a swim at Uncle Vince's pool, later,' Mum said. 'It's too warm for a walk in the hills today.'

'Bella doesn't want to walk anyway,' Sylvie said.

'No. She needs her rest. It won't be long, now.'

'Can I watch the puppies being born?'

'If you want to, yes. But they will probably come in the night when you are fast asleep. Most animals give birth in the darkness of night. Most people, too.'

'What time was I born?' Sylvie asked.

'Four minutes past midnight.' Mum smiled. She had a faraway look, as if she was remembering it all.

'Was Dad there?'

'Yes, he was. He was the first to hold you. Our perfect newborn daughter, with a head of dark hair.'

'Does it hurt?'

'Not the baby, but it hurts the mother sometimes. A *good* sort of pain, because it's the body working hard to help the baby out.'

'What does it feel like?'

'Hmmm. Hard to describe, Sylvie. A sort of tightening and squeezing. Coming in waves, closer and closer. Then you have to push. It's hard work, but it's natural enough. It's what our bodies are designed to do.'

Sylvie didn't want to think about it any more. She stood up. 'I'm going for a swim now,' she said.

'I'll be along in a while,' Mum said. 'Make sure Maria or Vince or the cousins are around before you go in the pool. Otherwise you must wait for me. And take a sun hat and sun-cream with you.'

'I know all that!' Sylvie said. 'You don't need to tell me every time.' The heat made her grumpy. She'd be better after a long swim.

At bedtime, the air was still warm. Sylvie stood outside on the terrace. Bats darted between the barn and the trees, their movements quicker and more jerky than birds'. They made a thin, high squeaking sound as they flew. Sylvie was the only one who could hear it: Mum said it was because she had *young ears*. Mum had been able to hear bat squeaks when *she* was ten, too.

Sylvie walked down the garden, away from the

house and all the lights, so she could see the stars more clearly. There were millions of them, tiny pinpricks of light travelling from such faraway stars that some had already burned up. Sylvie had watched a telly programme about it with Dad, back in the winter. And all these stars were just in their galaxy. There were thousands more galaxies, too far off to see even with the strongest telescope.

The moon rose over the mountains, golden at first and then turning pale and silvery as she watched it.

Bella paced the garden, round and round, and then she padded over to Sylvie and let her smooth her ears and rub the thick fur round her neck.

Sylvie walked across the grass to the shed. She picked up the old blue blanket in there and shook it out and put it back again, folding it neatly to make a comfortable bed for Bella.

Bella sat and watched her, panting heavily.

The garden was full of sounds: insects. Cicadas whirred and clicked from the bushes. White moths blundered from flower to flower.

'Sylvie?' Mum's voice drifted across the garden. 'Time to come in, now.'

'Night, night, Bella. Sleep tight.' Sylvie kissed her soft doggy head and smoothed her hand along her spine. She walked back towards the house, her bare feet leaving faint prints on the dewy grass.

Bella watched her go.

Chapter 7

✦

High in the sky now, the moon cast its huge silvery shadows over the garden. The air was cool and sweet. Bella paced restlessly round the grass, and then at last, as if she'd decided the time had come, she padded into the soft darkness of the shed, and lay down on the blanket.

The first puppy was born easily. It slithered out onto the blanket with a rush of liquid, and Bella licked and cleaned the puppy and bit the cord and licked the puppy some more, stirring it into taking its first breath. She nudged it towards the teats on her belly, so it could start to suck the first mouthfuls of milk. The puppy looked dark and smooth, with its rounded head and tiny ears and legs and tail, more like a damp rat than a puppy, but as its fur dried, it took on the silvery grey of moonlight, all except for a dark star on its head. Its eyes were tightly shut.

It would keep them closed for nearly two weeks. But it knew its mother already by her smell. The mother dog made gentle whimpering sounds, as if she were talking to her puppy all the time.

The mother dog's sides were heaving again, and she started panting fast. She strained her whole body, squeezing out the second pup. This time, although she licked and nudged the puppy, it did not move, or take a first breath. Try as she might, she could not stir life into this little one.

There were no more puppies.

Bella slept, and the one live puppy slept too, curled warm and safe against its mother's milky belly.

Chapter 8

❦

Sylvie cried in the morning when Gramps and Nonna told her what had happened.

'So there's just one?' she asked. 'One puppy, all alone?'

'Yes,' Nonna said. 'The little girl pup was too small to survive.'

'Nature has her reasons,' Gramps said. He sounded gruff, but he was sad too, underneath. Sylvie knew that because of the way he helped her dig a special place to bury the pup, and the tender way he wrapped it in a clean piece of cotton cloth and laid it on the earth. Afterwards, they planted poppy seeds on the place, to remember the puppy by. *Poppy*: that was the puppy's name, Sylvie decided.

'Now come and see the other pup,' Nonna said. 'Softly, now, so we don't upset Bella.'

Bella was lying on a clean towel, and the puppy was fast asleep, tucked close beside her. Bella thumped her tail on the floor, but she growled softly in her throat: a warning.

'She's never growled at me before,' Sylvie whispered.

'She's defending her baby,' Nonna said. 'It's a very strong instinct in a mother. Just stay quiet and don't go too close, and Bella will relax. She's still getting used to being a mum. Now, I've breakfast to get ready!' Nonna went back to the house.

Sylvie sat cross-legged on the grass and watched through the open doorway into the shed. The puppy would fit on one hand, it was so small. It was hard to see it properly because it was tucked up so close to Bella, but it looked as if its fur was a pale silver-grey all over, except for one dark star on its head. 'I shall call you Star,' Sylvie whispered.

'You don't look much like your mum,' Sylvie said to the pup. Perhaps that would change. Perhaps all puppies looked like this? Maybe its fur would change colour, the way a baby's hair sometimes got darker as the baby grew.

The pup burrowed under Bella, searching out the teats and as soon as it found one it latched on and started sucking. Its little grey bottom wriggled and its tiny front paws paddled against Bella's tummy. Sylvie loved the contented sucking sound it made. Everything about the puppy was so perfect and miniature. She watched and listened for ages, and Bella got used to her, and her soft talking.

Gramps came to sit next to her. 'Well, there's plenty of milk for that lucky pup, that's for sure. He'll be a big 'un.'

Bella wagged her tail, so it thumped against the wooden floor of the shed.

'He needs a name,' Gramps said. 'Have you thought of one?'

'I want to call him Star,' Sylvie said.

'Star.' Gramps said the word out loud. 'Yes, that will do.'

Nonna thought it was a lovely name. In Italian, the word for star was *stella*, but that sounded more like a girl's name. *Star* was much better for a boy pup.

'We should start handling him soon,' Nonna said. 'So he gets used to people.'

'Won't Bella mind?'

'Not now she's settled. She'll go for a little wander round the garden, soon, I expect, to stretch her legs, and we can have a better look at the pup.'

Sylvie helped herself to breakfast and took it all outside with her to eat so she could watch the puppy. Most of the time, Bella and the puppy slept. Bella lifted her head when Sylvie got up to take her bowl back to the kitchen, but she didn't follow her. Sylvie did her jobs for the morning: egg collection, first, then watering the red peppers and the tomatoes for Gramps. The sun was already hot, and it was just nine o'clock.

'Another scorcher,' Mum said. 'But I still want to go shopping, Nonna, if you're up for it? You going to come, Sylvie?'

'No thanks,' Sylvie said.

Gramps said he'd drive Mum and Nonna to the station. 'You're in charge, while I'm gone,' he said. 'I'll only be ten minutes, Sylvie. OK?'

Alone at the farmhouse, Sylvie pretended she really was in charge. She imagined this was her home all the time, and she worked on the land, growing vegetables, looking after hens. She'd have sheep or goats, maybe, and the new pup—Star—she'd train him up to be a proper herding dog. It calmed her down inside when she thought about living like that one day, when she was grown up. It made school and all that seem less important. She'd never be lonely because she'd have the animals. Star would be her own special dog; loyal and obedient to her. Holly could visit sometimes . . .

Bella yawned and stretched. She stood up and shook herself, and the puppy squeaked as it tumbled back onto the blanket.

'Careful, Bella!' Sylvie said.

Bella wagged her tail. She came over to Sylvie and put her head in her lap, waiting for Sylvie to stroke her head.

'Good dog,' Sylvie said. 'Clever Bella.' She smoothed her head, and stroked her neck the way she liked.

Bella shook herself and stretched again, and walked away. She did a wee under the pear tree and wandered around, sniffing the grass. She flumped down under the cherry tree and closed her eyes.

Perhaps she needs a rest, Sylvie thought, away from the puppy for a while.

The puppy was moving around on the blanket. It squirmed along on its tummy, not able to stand up on its legs properly yet. All the time it nosed around as if it was looking for Bella, or milk, or something.

Sylvie talked to the puppy, to calm him. 'It's OK, your mum's not gone far,' she told Star. She edged closer. She glanced back at Bella, but she didn't seem to mind, although she opened one eye when Sylvie went right inside the shed.

Sylvie crouched on the warm wooden floor, next to the blanket. She leaned over and gently touched the puppy with her finger, stroking along its small back. It was unbelievably soft! Sylvie looked back at Bella; she was still watching with one eye, but she seemed fine. Sylvie reached right in with both hands, and picked the puppy up gently, and put him on her lap.

She held her breath: he was so, so sweet. Tiny, and furry, and warm, snuffling and nuzzling her hand with his little blunt nose. She lifted him up, cradling him with both hands, and whispered into his tiny ears. 'I'm Sylvie, and you're Star, and you're going to be mine.' Perhaps if she wished it hard enough, it would become true.

Star stopped trembling. He nestled, warm and safe, cupped in Sylvie's hands. She felt a sudden flow of warmth and light flood her whole body. This was all she'd ever wanted.

A dog of her own.

Chapter 9

✦

August

Star changed a little every day. Sylvie ran down-stairs and out to the garden each morning as soon as she woke up, and there he was: a little stronger, a little less wobbly, looking more like a *dog*. Most of the time he was either sucking milk, or sleeping. But as he grew bigger, so the times he was awake got longer. He didn't mind being picked up. Sylvie held him and talked to him as much as she could. She talked to Bella too and brushed her fur and fed her three times a day, so that she could keep her strength up and make lots of milk for the puppy to drink. Bella took longer breaks: she walked off into the garden and left Sylvie in charge, keeping an eye on the puppy for her.

'Can I borrow your camera?' Sylvie asked Mum.

'Yes, if you're careful,' Mum said. 'What for?'

'I want to take lots of photos of Star as he grows. Like a sort of puppy diary. And I'm going to send some photos to Holly.'

'From Aunty Maria's computer?'

'Yes. If she says I can.'

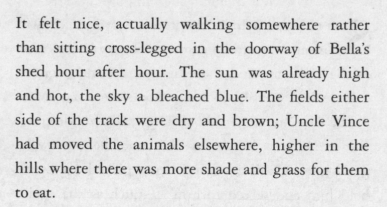

It felt nice, actually walking somewhere rather than sitting cross-legged in the doorway of Bella's shed hour after hour. The sun was already high and hot, the sky a bleached blue. The fields either side of the track were dry and brown; Uncle Vince had moved the animals elsewhere, higher in the hills where there was more shade and grass for them to eat.

Tobias came rushing out, barking at her, as she opened the gate. 'Hello, noisy dog!' She patted him and he rolled over so she'd stroke his furry belly.

Uncle Vince waved from the barn.

Sylvie waved back. She went into the farmhouse, Tobias still barking at her heels.

'*Ciao!*' she called out. 'Hello! It's me, Sylvie!'

'I'm in the kitchen!' Aunty Maria called back. She was chopping vegetables at the table: huge purple aubergines and red tomatoes, onions and garlic and courgettes. 'How is the puppy?' she asked Sylvie.

'He's very sweet and growing fast. Gramps thinks he'll be big. He has silver fur with gold bits in. I've brought Mum's camera.' Sylvie showed her the photos. 'Can we put them on the computer, please?'

Aunty Maria wiped her hands on her apron. '*Si!* Of course! I'll set it up for you, and you can get on with it, yes?'

Sylvie typed out an email to go with the photos.

Dear Holly, Here he is! Star. The sweetest
puppy in the world. So soft and furry. He has
huge paws so he will be a BIG dog when he
grows up. But at the moment he fits on two

hands. How are you? How was camping?

It's hot and sunny here now.

Miss you. xxx

She sent a second email, to Dad.

See you very soon! Look at this photo!

Love you. Sylvie xxxx

She attached the sweetest photo of Star feeding from Bella.

'All done!' she told Aunty Maria. 'Is it OK for me to swim, now?'

'Of course, my darling. I might join you when I've finished making lunch.'

Sylvie went into the bathroom to put on her swimsuit.

The surface of the pool was covered with half-drowned flies and beetles and other bugs. She went round with the net, scooping them out, before she got in properly for a swim. She floated on her back so she could think properly.

Writing those words to Holly had made her suddenly scared. *He will be a BIG dog*, she had written. She thought about the flat. The living room piled high with Dad's books. The tiny kitchen and her tiny bedroom. The stairs up and down. The busy roads. The long walk to the nearest park, where there was just a small football pitch of scrappy grass.

How could she possibly keep Star in a place like that?

Here, he was surrounded by meadows and woods and open space. Now, opening her eyes, she blinked at the brightness, and let her eyes adjust to the brilliance of the clear sky, the green hills going up into dark forest, and above the tree line, the bare rock of the high mountains.

She thought about Bella's life on the farm: the freedom she had to roam around. She imagined what it would be like for Bella, living in a city. It was cruel, wasn't it? To make a dog live in a tiny flat in London?

She flipped herself over again, onto her tummy, and started to swim again, up and down, to stop the thoughts crowding her head. But now she'd started thinking, she couldn't stop.

Chapter 10

❦

'What's the matter with Sylvie?' Nonna said to Mum.

Mum looked up from the book she was reading. 'Is there something? I hadn't noticed.'

'She's moping about like I don't know what!'

Mum laughed. 'She's a girl in luurve! She's in love with the puppy, that's all, Nonna.'

They didn't know she could hear them. She was sitting in her usual place, next to Bella's shed. Bella kept moving the puppy around, as if she wasn't happy with the nest she'd made with the blanket.

Nonna was still talking. Sylvie listened with one ear. She didn't like people talking about her. Even people who loved her, like Mum and Nonna.

'She's worried about something,' Nonna said.

Mum was quiet for a while, as if she was thinking. Then Sylvie heard her again. 'What on earth could she be worrying about? It's the summer holidays, she's in her favourite place with her favourite people, and there's a puppy to adore!'

'Maybe that's it . . . something to do with the puppy.' Nonna didn't say any more. Or if she did, Sylvie didn't hear.

Bella was carrying the puppy by the loose skin round his neck, bringing him right outside onto the grass.

Sylvie watched closely.

Bella put the puppy down on the grass right next to her. She nudged it with her nose, and then she went back into the shed. She was sorting out the blanket, tugging it with her teeth, as if she was trying to make it more comfortable.

The puppy squeaked for his mother. He didn't know where Bella had gone. He must sense the change, Sylvie thought: the garden must smell different from the warm shed. And even though his eyes were shut, maybe he could sense the brightness against his eyelids, the way you do when you close your eyes on a sunny day and it glows red on the inside.

He squirmed around, pushing himself along, until he found Sylvie's hand and he rested there, trembling slightly.

'It's fine, little one,' Sylvie told him. 'You're quite safe with me.'

Gently, she picked him up and put him on her lap. She stroked and soothed him. The puppy sniffed the air, he sniffed her cotton skirt and her hand; he butted it with his head and tried to suck her fingers. It tickled.

In the bright light of the garden, Sylvie saw how beautiful Star's fur was. How each silver hair ended in a tip of black, and how there were more red-gold hairs now, in the thicker fur around his neck and on his tail. She ran her finger over the dark star on his head, and along his little silken ears.

Star seemed to be creasing up his eyes. Perhaps it was too bright. Sylvie carried him over to the shade under the cherry tree. She sat down again with him on her lap.

Star moved his head. He made a tiny puppy whimper. He opened his eyes for the very first time.

Sylvie held her breath, watching.

He blinked. He shut them again. And then he tried again. Half opened them, widening his gaze.

His eyes were amazing. Nothing like Bella's shiny brown eyes. His eyes were blue, with a black pupil in the middle, a thin slit in the brightness.

Sylvie tried to imagine what it must be like, seeing the garden for the first time. Seeing her, and Bella, and the sky and sun and the whole world. How extraordinary, that a world that before was smells and tastes and touch was suddenly in colour and shape and form.

'Look, Gramps!' Sylvie called as he came past with the wheelbarrow. 'Star's opening his eyes!'

'Well I never!' Gramps squatted down next to Sylvie. He ran his hand over the puppy's silvery fur. 'He'll be standing strong and walking by the end of the week. And see: his teeth are already growing in there!' He showed Sylvie the little milk teeth in Star's mouth. '*Incisors*, they're called. He'll start chewing everything very soon.'

It was exciting, how quickly he was growing. She'd go and tell Holly about it later. She wouldn't think about what was going to happen when she went home at the end of the holidays. There were weeks to go, still. Dad would be arriving at the weekend.

Bella waddled over and flopped down in the shade. Sylvie put the puppy down next to her so he could feed again. The puppy grunted and squeaked like a plump piglet as he sucked hard on the teat. Bella groaned and rolled over a bit more. She stretched out her head and closed her eyes as if she was bored with feeding a puppy who was always hungry.

Sylvie went to fetch the egg basket.

'Star's opened his eyes! They're blue,' she told Nonna in the kitchen. 'And he's getting teeth!'

'Now the fun will start,' Nonna said. 'I remember Bella as a pup, into everything and chewing everyone's shoes. A right song and dance!'

'But you liked having her. She wasn't much trouble, was she?' Sylvie was anxious again. She didn't want Nonna remembering the difficult bits about having a puppy.

'Gramps took her on, so he trained her. It takes a lot of time and patience,' Nonna said. 'She was a working dog, remember. She went everywhere with him, then. She still does, when you aren't here, Sylvie. And maybe it's in the genes: perhaps Star will be a good working dog too, when he's older.'

The squirmy feeling was there again, deep in her belly. Star wasn't meant to be a working dog. He was *her* dog.

If Nonna started thinking about him like that, next thing, she'd be wondering about giving him to someone on a farm who needed a working dog.

'He's nothing like Bella,' Sylvie said. 'Anyone can see that. He's like his father.'

Nonna laughed. 'And who might that be, I wonder? That's anyone's guess.'

Sylvie went in the van with Mum and Gramps to meet Dad at Pisa airport, even though it was too hot to be in the van for long. They stopped at the river on the way there, and at a café just inside the big city walls in Lucca on the way back.

Dad was excited to be in Italy again. 'There's nowhere like it for coffee!' He kissed Mum again. 'Or for beautiful women!'

Mum laughed and hit him playfully with the menu. 'Stop that, immediately!'

'I meant you!' Dad protested.

'Yes? And the waitress.' Mum's eyes shone bright with happiness. Sylvie hadn't noticed how much Mum missed Dad, until now. It was nice, seeing them together, but it made her feel a bit left out. She was glad Gramps was there too. She let him have a lick of her raspberry ice cream and she had one of his: coffee and almond.

'Which is best?' Gramps asked her.

'Definitely raspberry.'

Back at the house, Gramps opened a bottle of wine and Nonna brought out freshly baked bread and a dish of huge green olives. The grown ups settled round the table to talk.

'Come and see Star, first!' Sylvie tugged Dad's hand, to make him come with her.

Bella and the puppy were lying on the sun-warmed grass just outside the shed. Dad hunkered down for a better look. 'Just one pup. All alone!' Dad smiled. 'A bit like you, Sylvie.'

'Nothing like me!' Sylvie said. 'I haven't got silver fur and blue eyes.'

Dad laughed.

'But isn't he sweet?' Sylvie wished Dad would concentrate properly on Star. 'Isn't he the most beautiful puppy you've ever seen? And he's no trouble at all. Bella's such a good mum.'

Dad looked at her. 'Oh, Sylvie,' he said, in a sad voice.

'What?'

'It's just ... never mind.' Dad stood up and stretched out his back. He smiled at Sylvie again. She knew he was going to change the subject. 'I've brought you a stack of new books to read. Just in case you're getting bored with no one to play with. Missing Holly and your other friends.'

'I've got Bella and Star, remember?'

'I'm going back to have my glass of wine, now,' Dad said. 'I've been looking forward to this moment for weeks. Let's have a walk together, in the morning. Just you and me, Sylvie. Yes?'

'OK,' Sylvie said.

She didn't want to sit around talking for hours with the grown-ups. She decided she'd go up to the farm to email Holly. Maybe she'd look up what it said about *puppy development* again. She wanted to know *everything*. So she'd be properly prepared. She'd have an answer for everything Dad said about why she couldn't keep Star. She just knew that was what he was planning to say to her tomorrow, on their walk.

Hello, Holly. Star opened his eyes today.
They are blue but Gramps says they will change
as he gets older. He is almost walking properly
and he has tiny teeth. He yelps and squeaks.
Dad's just arrived so we'll do more holiday things
now like walks and the beach.
How are you?
Please email me back soon. Xxx

There were hundreds of sites about puppy development and training. It took ages, reading them on line. Her eyes started feeling tired.

Eventually, Aunty Maria said she had better go home. 'They'll be missing you! It will be dinner time, and Nonna won't like you being late.'

Chapter 11

❦

Last week in August

Star's eyes weren't blue any more.

At first, it was as if there were specks of gold in the blue, and then the blue itself seemed to fade. And this morning, Sylvie suddenly saw as they came into the sunny garden, Star's eyes looked completely yellow-gold, all except for the black slit of the pupil in the middle, narrowed against the bright light.

He could walk and run and his ears stood up straight now, all except the very tips. He played and followed Bella about. He followed Sylvie too, and the hens. He was beginning to eat little bits of meat, and feeding less from Bella. His head and his feet looked much too big for his body. Sometimes he tripped over his own paws. He was sweet and funny, and his teeth were sharp as needles. He wanted to chew everything: shoes, bare toes, fingers. Sylvie's job was to look after him, keeping him safe, playing with him and making sure he didn't get under Nonna's feet.

Everyone had been really busy the last two weeks. Gramps was harvesting vegetables most days, taking them to the market at Castelnuovo to sell. Nonna and Mum had collected honey from the beehives in the top of the flower meadow and put it into jars. Dad and Mum and Sylvie had been to the sea several times, and for long walks in the hills, and now Dad had gone home and Mum and Sylvie only had one week left before they went back too, for the beginning of the new school term.

'Morning, Sylvie,' Gramps said as he came out of the back door.

'Have you seen Star's eyes?' Sylvie asked him.

'What's wrong with them?'

'Nothing. They look amazing. They've totally changed. Come here, Star!' She patted her legs with her hands to call him, and he bounded over, tumbling over his too-big paws.

'Sit, Star!' Sylvie said firmly. She pushed him down, so he was sitting, but he wouldn't stay still for long. He wanted to play.

'He's a lively one,' Gramps said. 'You've done a good job looking after him, Sylvie, while we've been so busy.' He crouched down, so he could look at Star's eyes.

The puppy blinked in the sunshine and pulled his head away.

'Well I never,' Gramps said. 'There's a thing. Would you believe it! I've not seen anything like that for a long time. Star's got wolf eyes.'

'What do you mean?' Sylvie asked.

'Yellow eyes like that. The daddy dog . . . not a *dog* as such at all, I reckon. That's why Bella came back in such a state. Why she was gone for so many days. Why the pup's so big.'

Sylvie still didn't understand.

'I reckon Star's father might have been a *wolf*. Which means Star could be a *wolf-dog pup*. It happens, from time to time. There have been others, on farms near the mountains.'

Sylvie tried to take it in. What did it mean, exactly?

Half Bella, half wolf . . .

Would Star grow up too fierce and big? She watched him as he ran over the grass, tugging at the old shoe he played with as a toy. He looked so small and furry and cuddly. Perhaps Gramps was wrong.

Gramps frowned.

'What's the matter?' Sylvie asked. 'Why are you looking so serious?'

'It's very hard to train a wolf-dog pup, Sylvie. They're more than half wild. The wolf nature is strong. It's not such good news for Star. It'll be very hard to find him a home.'

For a moment, Sylvie couldn't speak at all.

Her voice came out funny, as if her throat was too dry. 'But Star's home is here! With Bella. With me, and you and Nonna. How can you even *think* of giving him away to anyone else? Gramps!' Sylvie's eyes stung with tears. She turned her head away so Gramps wouldn't see.

Had Gramps been planning to give Star away, all along? Been looking for another home for him, with strangers? Wasn't it obvious to everyone that Star belonged to *her*?

And now what? If Star really was more *wolf* than *dog*?

'Have you collected the eggs, Sylvie?' Mum called from the back door. 'Nonna needs them.'

'Better get on,' Gramps said. 'Work to be done.'

He hadn't answered her question.

Sylvie went round the garden, searching out hidden eggs in the usual places. Star followed her, getting in the way, trying to play and nibbling her bare toes. In the end, she had to put him in the shed while she collected the eggs. She could hear him whining, scratching at the door.

She felt sorry for him.

She felt sorry for the hens, too, laying eggs every day and hiding them cleverly under the spinach or behind the compost bin, and still every day she found them and took them away. They'd never be able to hatch out a brood of chicks.

Suddenly *everything* seemed cruel and unfair.

Nonna looked up as Sylvie went into the kitchen with the basket of eggs. 'What's the matter, Sylvie? You look all upset.'

'Gramps says Star might be a wolf-dog pup,' Sylvie said. 'And no one will want him, and I'm GLAD because he's MY puppy.' She didn't mean to sound so cross, but suddenly she was. She ran out of the kitchen, before Nonna could say anything. She ran out of the back door, and started walking, fast, up the track, the way she usually walked with Bella.

Sylvie went by herself. She didn't care what Mum or Nonna said.

She half-walked, half-ran through the flower meadow, and along the ridge to the beginning of the chestnut woods. She climbed up the steep stone mule path, zigzagging between the trees. It was cool and fresh still in the deep shade. She began to feel better, walking in the green light filtering through chestnut and beech leaves. As she got higher, the wind in the trees made a different sound, a sighing and rushing like water rather than air through leaves.

She stopped to get her breath back. The sounds and smells of the forest soothed her. She sat on a moss-covered stone, her back against a tree trunk, and let the tears come at last.

I need a plan, she thought. I need to show them I can look after Star, and teach him to behave. I can't take him back to London, but maybe I can keep him here, and every holiday I can train him and then he will be safe and happy and Nonna and Gramps won't mind.

She carried on climbing, up out of the trees and onto the grass and rocks of the mountain. Her heart beat fast. It was hotter here. She should have brought water to drink. She carried on climbing. She came over a ridge and surprised a herd of wild goats; they careered away and then stopped to watch her, their big horns silhouetted against the sky.

Sylvie thought about the wolf living somewhere on these mountains who had fathered Star. She imagined meeting him: one lone silver wolf with yellow eyes, staring back at her. Or perhaps he was the leader of a whole pack . . . she imagined them, running silently along the ridge. It would be truly amazing, to see that. In all her years of coming here, she'd never seen them. But Uncle Vince had. Uncle Vince hated the wolves, because sometimes in spring they came down into the valley to take the young lambs. Or so he said. When Uncle Vince walked in the forest and mountains, sometimes he carried a gun, even though the wolves were supposed to be protected.

Fear rippled down her spine.

She wouldn't think about that now.

Chapter 12

❦

In her head, as she walked back down the mule-path, Sylvie was writing the email she was going to send to Holly.

> Gramps thinks Star's father was a wild mountain wolf! His eyes are yellow-gold: wolf eyes.

The actual words, put like that, made her shiver with excitement. It made Star *extra* special, whatever Gramps said. She imagined herself walking with Star through this forest; he would look amazing, his muscles rippling under his thick silver fur. She would have her hand on his tall back, and they would be inseparable. She would be a girl who walks with a wolf, like in a story. She would tame him completely, and he would trust her and be her faithful companion.

She remembered, suddenly, the book with the blue wolf on the cover she'd half read in the bookshop back in June.

She came out of the shade and into the sun-drenched meadow. The grass was parched and dry, more like hay. The sun beat down on her head. She was so thirsty. It felt as if she'd been gone for hours and hours.

Now she was at the track, she could see Mum,

hanging out the washing, pegging sheets along the line stretched across the top part of the garden. Star was tugging at the sheet, giving little whimpers and yelps. Bella slept on her side in the shade.

'Star!' she called. 'Here, Star!'

He ran up to her, tail wagging, as she came into the garden. He was still so little and furry and sweet. He was nothing like a wolf. Perhaps Gramps was wrong, after all.

'Hello, Sylvie. Have you been at the farm?' Mum asked. 'Sending photos to Holly?'

Sylvie didn't answer Mum's questions. She didn't

want to lie, exactly. 'I need a drink!' she said instead. 'It's so hot.'

'Didn't you swim at Uncle Vince's?' Mum asked.

'No.' That at least was true.

'I want to get a book about training a puppy,' Sylvie blurted out. 'I want to start training Star properly.'

Mum stopped pegging out a bright blue towel and looked at Sylvie.

'Sylvie, darling,' she said. 'You know we can't possibly take Star back home with us, don't you? I know you'd love a dog. But the flat—'

'Is too small. We don't have a garden. You're at work all day,' Sylvie said. 'And Star would be miserable in a city. I know, Mum. But I could keep him here. There's loads of space. Star can live with Bella and share her shed. Nonna and Gramps will hardly notice another dog.'

'I don't think that's true, Sylvie.' Mum frowned. 'We can't expect Nonna and Gramps to take on more work. They've got enough to do already. It costs money, feeding a dog. Vets' bills. All that. And a normal puppy needs lots of attention. Imagine how much more for a half wild puppy.'

So Mum knew. Gramps must have told her already.

'I can look after him and train him when I'm here,' Sylvie said. 'Same as I do with Bella.'

'Bella is a grown-up dog. She's perfectly behaved. Gramps trained her when she was a pup. And she's not half wolf.'

'Star might not be, either. We don't know for sure!' Sylvie said. 'It's too soon to tell.'

Mum sighed. 'I know how much you want to keep him. But it's not that simple. There are weeks and months, even, when you aren't here. Especially in the winter. Think of that.'

Sylvie felt herself getting hotter and hotter. 'I wish I *was* here,' she shouted. 'I wish I could be here all the time, with Nonna and Gramps instead of horrible YOU in horrible London! I hate living in two places. I hate you!'

She couldn't stop herself. Hot tears spilled down her face. She ran, shaking, across to the house, and up the stairs to her room.

She lay down on the bed, still shaking with sobs. Her chest hurt. She was too hot, and exhausted, and furious with Mum and Gramps and *everyone*.

Nonna had pulled the shutters over to keep the room

dark and cool. Sylvie drank the rest of the water in the glass on the bedside table. That made her feel a bit better. She lay on her bed for ages, eyes open in the darkened room, trying to work out what to do now.

Nonna loved her.

Nonna would understand about wanting something so much you can't let it go.

If she could get Nonna on her side . . .

She began to feel a tiny bit hopeful again.

Sounds of a normal summer day drifted up from the garden. Birds sang from the trees. Cicadas chirred. Honey bees buzzed in the lavender bush below her window. Further away, a tractor rumbled up the track.

She'd have to talk to Nonna when she was on her own, so Mum or Gramps wouldn't interfere. When Nonna wasn't too busy doing things. After her nap, in the afternoon, perhaps. If not today, tomorrow, or the next day. There were six days left.

Chapter 13

❧

Hi, Sylvie. Thank you for your
amazing photos. How cool is it about
Star being half WOLF!!!! I wish I
could come and see him for real!
It is raining again today 😞 There
is nothing to do here. Will you get
to keep him? Has your mum said yes?
Can't wait to see you!!
Love Holly xxxxx

Sylvie couldn't bear to write back and tell Holly
that Mum was still saying NO. She shut down the

computer without sending a reply. She got down off Aunty Maria's desk chair, and went home without speaking to anyone.

Nonna was shelling peas at the table. She looked smaller, older, when Sylvie saw her like that, unexpectedly, from a distance. She was wearing a faded blue wrap-around apron, and her hair looked faded too, as if Nonna had been in the sun too much.

Sylvie came across the front garden. Bella and Star were curled up near the table, both sleeping. Bella wagged her tail but didn't bother to get up.

'Come help me, Sylvie darling,' Nonna said. When she smiled, her face was all crinkly, and her eyes shone dark, like Sylvie's own eyes.

Sylvie slid into a chair next to Nonna. She picked up a pod from the big pile on the table and slit it with her fingernail up the ridged side till it popped open. Inside, there were nine perfect round peas, bright green. She always counted how many.

She let the peas ping into the metal colander. She picked up another pod.

Neither of them spoke.

It made her feel comfortable and safe, sitting next to Nonna, shelling peas like this. One, and another, and the next. They worked in a rhythm, and the peas made a ping sound each time they hit the metal sides of the colander. The pile of empty pods got higher, and the full pod pile went down, smaller and smaller, until they were all done.

'Perfect,' Nonna said. '*Grazie.*' Thank you.

They stayed sitting there, side by side, even though they had finished the job.

'Your mamma has gone with Gramps to the market,' Nonna said. 'So we can please ourselves.' She got up from her chair stiffly, making a funny little noise as if her back hurt. She carried the full colander back with her into the house.

Sylvie sat and waited.

Nonna came back out. She put a tray down on the table: two glasses of home-made lemonade and two slices of cake on a flowery plate. She sat down again next to Sylvie.

'It is very hard,' Nonna said softly, 'when there is something you want so bad, and you can't have it. Like, your heart is breaking.'

Sylvie didn't say a word.

'I thought my heart would break when your mamma met your father the Englishman, from

London. When she told me she was going to marry him, and live with him in England. This, I had never dreamed would happen to my child. My beautiful daughter.

'But you see, it turns out fine. We *compromise*. She lives in London, she has her job, and your dad and you. But she comes back home to us every holiday. She brings you with her. We have not lost our daughter, or our grand-daughter, after all.'

Sylvie held her breath. Nonna had more to say. She listened.

'So, you want a dog so much it breaks your heart that you can't have one in London. But we can compromise. We keep Star for you, here, and when you come, he is all your dog, your responsibility.'

'Really?' Tears welled up in Sylvie's eyes.

Nonna understood everything. She knew Sylvie so well, she didn't even have to ask.

'Are you really sure?'

Nonna nodded.

'Even though he might be a wolf-dog pup?' Sylvie asked.

'Yes, even that. Well, no one else will want him,' Nonna said. 'And what are we to do? He is here now, and we must make things work as best we can. But you will have to work hard to train him. Gramps will help you. And a dog is not a toy, or something you can lose interest in later. It's for his whole life, Sylvie, however long that is. Are you sure you want to do that?'

'Yes,' Sylvie said. 'I am sure. I promise, Nonna.'

'Now, let me give you a big hug, and then we will eat cake! And later, you must make your peace with your mamma! Don't be angry with her, Sylvie.'

Gramps dumped two bags of shopping on the table. 'Have a look in the smaller bag, Sylvie.'

Sylvie pulled out a brown leather collar with a silver disc. She turned it over so she could read the lettering engraved on the disc. *Star,* it said, and then a phone number, and the name of the farmhouse. The leather collar felt stiff and new in her hands.

'Thank you, Gramps.' She hugged him. 'Thank you so much for letting me keep him.'

'It'll be hard work, mind,' Gramps said. 'Your mother's not best pleased.'

'She'll come round,' Nonna said. 'She's only trying to think about what's best for everyone.'

'She thinks we spoil you,' Gramps said. 'Maybe we do!'

Star sat up, his eyes still sleepy. He yawned, and stretched, and wagged his little tail.

'Here, Star,' Sylvie called to him. She held out her hand.

He waddled over, sniffed her hand, licked it and made her laugh.

'Now sit,' Sylvie said. She pressed his furry bottom to make him sit down, but he wouldn't stay sitting. He tugged at the edge of her skirt with his teeth, as if he wanted her to play with him.

'Let go, Star.'

'Good,' Gramps said. 'Be clear who is in charge. Mean what you say. Keep your voice steady and low.' He helped hold Star still while Sylvie fastened the collar round his neck.

He didn't like it one bit. He ducked and twisted and tried to pull it off. He turned his head, to try to bite the collar, and when he couldn't, he rubbed his head along the grass to try and push it off.

Sylvie felt sad, watching him.

'He'll get used to it, in time,' Gramps said. 'When he's happy enough with the collar, we'll try a lead on him.'

'Why?' Sylvie asked. 'Bella never goes on a lead.'

'She did when she was a pup. And sometimes she still does, if we take her to town. It's all part of training Star, Sylvie. He needs to learn to do exactly what he's told.'

Star whimpered. He sat down and scratched himself with his back leg, and nearly toppled over. He sat back, lifted his head, and howled.

Mum came out of the house. She watched anxiously. 'Are you sure this is going to work?'

Sylvie turned away. It was hard seeing Star so unhappy. She wished she could take the collar off again.

'We'll take him for a walk with us, later,' Gramps said. 'He's old enough to go a short distance, now. He'll like that. Bella, too.'

They waited until the early evening, when the air started to cool down a little. Sylvie was excited. Her first walk with her own puppy! Her heart beat faster as she fastened Bella's old lead to Star's collar.

Away from the safety of the garden, Star was unsure. He stayed close to Bella, padding behind her so closely that when she stopped still he bumped into her and she turned and nipped him with her teeth, irritated. He was nervous: a bee made him jump, and when Uncle Vince went up the track on the tractor, he lay down in the grass, hiding, shivering, his ears back and his eyes alert.

Sylvie talked to him the whole time, to reassure him. 'You're safe with us, Star!' she said. She held his lead slack, so it would not pull on the collar and hurt him. Gradually, he relaxed. Bella walked faster, ahead now with Gramps, and Star came on behind, distracted by passing butterflies, stopping to sniff at things every few seconds. Sylvie tugged gently at the lead to make him walk on.

They walked as far as the beginning of the forest; the puppy was tired. He kept sitting down. Bella had already gone far ahead, trotting up the mule path as if she was happy to be going for a proper walk after weeks of staying at home.

'Bella!' Sylvie called. 'Wait there!'

For a second Sylvie thought Bella was going to keep on walking up the hill.

Star watched her too, his ears pricked, straining at the lead. He whined anxiously. It was more than he could bear, Sylvie thought: watching his mother disappear. He yelped and cried. Sylvie knelt down to comfort him. But it was Bella he wanted, not her.

Bella couldn't bear it either. She turned and hurried back down the path towards them, wagging her tail. As soon as she came close, Star whimpered and nuzzled her and wagged his tiny tail. Bella licked his face and he licked hers back.

'See that?' Gramps said. 'That's how well bonded they are at the moment, mother and pup. That will change as the pup grows. Bella will get more and more fed up with him. And the pup needs to bond with a person, instead, if he is to be a good house dog. It should be you, really, but we will have to share it, since you can't be here all the time.'

Sylvie looked at him. 'It will be all right, won't it?' she asked, anxiously.

'We'll do the best we can,' Gramps said. 'That's all anyone can do.'

It didn't make her feel better. A worry knot came in her belly, and it wouldn't go away.

It stayed right to the end of the holiday, when she had to say goodbye to Nonna and Gramps, to Bella and Star.

Sylvie held her puppy close. She could feel his little heart beating under her hand. He wriggled and squirmed and struggled to get down. She kissed the soft fur on the top of his head. 'Please be good, Star,' she whispered. 'I'll come back as soon as I can.'

Gramps started up the engine.

'Time to go, Sylvie,' Mum said. 'We mustn't miss that plane. Give Star to Nonna, now.'

Nonna took Star from her and held him tight while they got into the van. 'I'll take care of him for you, darling,' Nonna said. 'Don't worry. Have a safe journey!'

Sylvie couldn't bear to look at her, or wave, or say anything.

'Thanks for a wonderful summer,' Mum called. 'See you again soon!'

And already they were off, the van gathering speed, the farmhouse behind them getting smaller and smaller.

Chapter 14

❦

London: September

Sylvie had been back in London for two weeks. School had started again. She was in the top class now, with a new teacher. But today was Saturday, and Sylvie and Holly were sitting upstairs in the book-shop, piles of books about puppies and dogs around them. Sylvie was half-listening to what was happening downstairs.

Dad was talking to a man. Even from up here, Sylvie could hear the worry in Dad's voice as he answered the man's questions. The man was called Mr Harding; she knew he owned this building. Dad had to pay him rent for the bookshop.

'This one looks good.' Holly held up a book to show Sylvie. 'It's about a different way of training a puppy. Like horse whispering, but for dogs.' She frowned, and it made her nose wrinkle up. 'You have to understand the dog's *body language*!'

Sylvie smiled. 'What does *that* mean?'

Holly showed her the page. 'It says you have to notice what it's doing. And work out what it's feeling like. So, in the morning when it gets up and is dashing about, it needs to do a wee! So, you let it out. And it learns to wee outside, not in the house. Or something like that. You have to respect the puppy, and love it and understand it, instead of *commanding* it.'

'Gramps wouldn't agree,' Sylvie said. 'In any case, Star doesn't live in the house. And he already knows about weeing outside, because he copies Bella.'

It had gone quiet downstairs. Mr Harding must have gone.

She turned another page in the big hardback book on her lap. It was about wolves, with big glossy photos. She was reading the chapter about wolf pup development.

8–10 weeks. Adults abandon den and move pups. Weaning complete. 12 weeks: begin to accompany adults on hunting trips for a short while.

She studied the photograph. The wolf pups looked just like Star. *Weaning complete* meant the pups stopped drinking milk from the mum, and ate meat instead. Her eyes kept going over the line about *hunting*.

She imagined Star, running around in Nonna and Gramps's garden.

Nonna had sent her an email that morning with a photo of Star.

> He is getting bigger every day. Bella is bored with him, now. She leaves him and goes off by herself. He needs other puppies, really, to play with. This morning he's been chasing the hens!

Nonna hadn't said anything more, but Sylvie could imagine the rest. Gramps would be cross. Nonna might have to shut Star in the shed, or tie him up.

She told Holly about the email. 'I should be there, to play with him,' she said.

'Well, you can't be,' Holly said. 'There's no point worrying about it all the time!' She put the book back on the pile on the carpet. 'Shall we go and do something else, now?'

'Like what?'

Holly shrugged. 'I dunno. We could go back to my house, if you want? Make pizzas for lunch. I've got to clean out the guinea pigs.'

'OK.' Sylvie stood up. 'We'd better tidy up here otherwise Dad'll go mental.'

They put the books back on the shelves in the right places.

'We'd make good librarians!' Holly said.

They went downstairs. The shop was getting busier now; people were browsing along the shelves. Dad looked up from the till and smiled. 'OK, you two?'

'We're going to Holly's,' Sylvie told him. 'Can you collect me, later?'

'Not till after six,' Dad said. 'Phone your mum, if you need to come home before that.'

Sylvie sat on the grass in Holly's garden, two fat ginger-haired guinea pigs on her lap. Holly was cleaning out the hutches, sweeping out the old sawdust and hay and filling them with fresh. Every time one of the guinea pigs tried to escape off Sylvie's lap, she pulled it back, smoothing it with her hand. They chuntered and squeaked, as if they were talking. They were furry and sweet, with their beady eyes and twitching noses. But they were a tiny bit boring. It wasn't like having your own dog.

Sylvie thought about Star. How might a guinea pig look to him? She knew, really. If he were here now, he'd be chasing them round the garden, like he chased the hens, and then one snap of his mouth and they'd be . . . lunch! Guiltily, she stroked their furry backs.

'Ready,' Holly said. 'Put them back in the hutch now, if you want.'

The guinea pigs burrowed under the fresh straw, squeaking loudly. It was probably the most exciting thing that ever happened to them, getting new hay, Sylvie thought.

Marmalade the cat wove himself round Holly's legs, and then round Sylvie's. She bent down to scratch him behind his ears. A cat was better than a guinea pig, as pets go. But nothing like a dog. She didn't tell Holly any of that, of course.

'Tree-house?' Holly said.

Sylvie nodded.

'We'll get some food to take up, first.'

Holly's mum was in the kitchen, pulling armfuls of wet washing out of the machine into a plastic basket. She looked up and smiled at Sylvie. 'All right, love?'

'Yes thanks,' Sylvie said.

'You two can hang this lot out for me on the line.'

Holly groaned. 'Why do we have to? You never make Alfie do anything!'

'I don't mind,' Sylvie said. She really didn't. At home, the washing had to go in the tumble drier, or be draped all round the flat on the radiators. It was nice pegging things up on a line outside, so the clothes flapped and waved in the wind. It felt old-fashioned, in a nice way.

'Urgh, yuck!' Holly said, holding a pair of blue boxers by one corner. 'I don't see why Alfie can't hang out his own smelly stuff.'

'Where is Alfie?' Sylvie asked. 'I haven't seen him for ages.'

'Out. Or still asleep. Either one or the other. He's never just *around*, like a normal person. I'm never going to be like Alfie, even when I'm sixteen.'

Sixteen was practically grown up. Sylvie tried to imagine Holly and herself, being sixteen, but it was too hard. She hung out the last of the bundle of blue socks and put the peg bag back in the basket.

'There's pizza, if you want to put it in the oven for lunch,' Holly's mum said. 'What are your family doing today, Sylvie?'

'Dad's working in the shop. Mum's doing school stuff.'

'Well, it's nice to see you. Holly missed you in the summer.'

They carried their slices of pizza over to the tree. Sylvie climbed up first and settled herself in Holly's tree-house.

'Shove up a bit,' Holly said from the top of the ladder. 'So I can get in too!'

Sylvie shuffled along a bit on her bottom, her legs dangling down from the platform edge. 'I'll fall out, if I move any more.'

It was funny remembering how much space there had been when it was first built, when they'd only been about seven years old. Things changed but so gradually you didn't notice, until suddenly, like now, you did!

'What was your dad going on about, earlier?' Holly asked. 'At the bookshop, talking to that man.'

'He's the person who owns the bookshop building. He wants to sell it.'

Holly wrinkled her nose. 'Is that good or bad?'

'I don't know. Bad, if someone buys it, and wants to turn it into something else. Like, not a bookshop. But good if Dad could buy it. Only we don't have enough money, I don't think.' That worry knot in her belly seemed to pull tighter. She'd heard Mum and Dad talking about it, late into the night.

'Oh well.' Holly licked the tomato sauce off her fingers, one by one in turn. 'I expect it will turn out all right. There's nothing you can do about it anyway.'

Holly was always cheerful like that, Sylvie thought. Maybe it was easier to be cheerful when you lived in a big house with a garden and lots of pets and enough money so your parents didn't talk about it over and over.

'It's only one month till my birthday,' Holly said out of the blue. 'Shall I have a party again? Or do something else?'

Sylvie thought for a bit. 'We could go somewhere, instead of a party. Like, the seaside for a day. Or an excursion. Where might you like to go?'

Holly shrugged. 'I dunno. A circus, maybe? Or a film?'

Sylvie remembered going to a circus when she was younger, when they'd been camping in France on the long drive down to Italy. It was exciting and terrible, both at the same time. An old-fashioned sort of circus with animals: you weren't allowed to do that in England any more, because it was cruel, how they trained the animals. But there was a sort of thrill when she saw the lions, first in cages, at the edge of the field near the big tent, and then in the show itself: three lionesses, running in circles round the ring, and jumping from one platform to another, and the ringmaster flicking a whip, talking to them the whole time. There had been horses too: a tiny white one and a tall black one with wild eyes, and girls in spangled costumes balanced on their bare backs, their arms wide, like ballerinas. Worst of all was the elephant: slow, beautiful, with its calm wise eyes, being made to do things that made it look silly, like stand with its front legs on an upturned bucket, and sway to music. She had watched with tears running down her face. It seemed the saddest thing she had ever seen: an elephant dancing for a stupid man in a red coat.

Sylvie sat with her arms round her hunched-up knees and listened to Holly talking about school, and friends—who to invite and all that. There was a boy she liked; but could you just ask one boy? Zak . . . Holly's voice rattled on, and Sylvie said yes and no at the right places, but her heart wasn't in it.

She kept thinking about Star. She couldn't stop herself. What would happen if he kept on chasing things? What if it got worse? It was weeks till she could go to Italy. Gramps didn't have enough time to spend training a puppy. And supposing there wasn't going to be enough money to pay for so many trips to Italy? She'd heard Dad saying something to Mum about *holidays*, even though she couldn't catch exactly what.

'You're not listening!' Holly said. 'What's the matter with you today?'

'Sorry,' Sylvie said. 'Nothing.'

'You're a worry guts,' Holly said. 'You're thinking about Star, aren't you?'

'I can't help it.'

They watched Holly's brother Alfie walk out of the kitchen door and slump down at the garden table with a mug of coffee. He got out his mobile phone and started texting.

Holly giggled. 'We could drop something on his head,' she whispered. 'He doesn't know we're here.'

Sylvie felt shy, suddenly. Alfie was good looking, she supposed, with his dark hair flopping in his eyes. She wondered what it would be like to have a big brother. She didn't know anything at all about boys, really. Apart from the ones in her class, of course.

'I know you're up there, Hol,' Alfie said without looking up.

Holly chucked a dried seed at him. It hit the back of his neck.

'Ha ha,' he said sarcastically. 'Grow up, Holly. Get a life.'

'Like you?' Holly laughed.

Marmalade jumped up onto the table. Alfie scratched the cat under its chin. The cat rolled over so he could stroke its belly. The cat seemed to think Alfie was nice enough, Sylvie thought, and animals know about people.

'I think I'll go home, now,' she said. 'Can I call Mum?'

'When will they let you have your own phone?' Holly asked.

'Next year, when we go to secondary school. Only you have to be careful, they can give you brain cancer.'

Holly laughed. 'What, a mobile phone? There you go again! Honestly, Sylvie!'

'It's true. It was on the news!'

'They make most of it up,' Holly said. 'That's what Dad says. You shouldn't believe any of it.'

They climbed down the ladder, going carefully backwards. Alfie smiled at Sylvie as she ran past. It was silly to be scared of him, Sylvie knew. She was a bit scared of her grown-up cousins too, Uncle Vince's boys. They'd be there at Christmas this year.

'What are you going to do now?' Holly asked her in the kitchen while they waited for Mum to turn up.

'I'm going to email Nonna. And read some more things about wolves.'

The car drew up outside in the street and Mum beeped the horn to make Sylvie hurry up. There wasn't anywhere to park.

'Thanks for having me!' Sylvie called out to Holly's mum. She hugged Holly. 'See you Monday!' and ran down the steps to the waiting car.

Chapter 15

October

Once a week, usually at the weekend, Nonna sent an email to Sylvie. Sometimes she sent a photograph of Star, too, so Sylvie could see how much he had grown. He was almost as big as Bella now, but thinner and with longer legs and much bigger paws.

This Monday, before she left for school, Sylvie turned on the computer in the living room to see if there was a new message from Nonna.

She imagined her walking up the track to Uncle Vince's farm, going into the back room where Aunty Maria kept the computer, and slowly tapping out the words with one finger.

No, nothing from Nonna, yet. Sylvie looked through all the old messages she'd saved, instead.

September 14th

Star is growing faster than ever!

He is full of energy and mischief.

September 21st

Gramps has made a wire netting fence to keep the hens safe. Star is so naughty we can't trust him not to chase them.

September 30th

Last night we heard him howling from the shed. Gramps locks him up there now. We are a bit concerned he might run off.

October 7th

Bella's getting bad-tempered because Star won't leave her alone: he tries to make her play and wrestle with him. Poor Bella! She thinks she's too old to play.

Nonna didn't exactly *say* she wished they hadn't kept the puppy, but she didn't sound very happy, Sylvie thought. She still hadn't shown any of the emails to Mum or Dad. She was worried they might say *it's too much work for Nonna and Gramps* . . . Or, *we'll have to find a new home for Star* . . .

'Are you nearly ready, Sylvie?' Mum called from the kitchen. 'We need to be off in five minutes.'

Sylvie clicked on *New message*. She started to type.

It won't be long till I can come and help, Nonna. I can play with Star and start training him to be better behaved. I have read all about it in some books. I am sorry he is being a bother.

Sylvie read back what she'd written. It wasn't Star's fault he was a wolf-dog pup. If he were in the wild, he'd have other pups to play with, and he'd have lots of space to run off his energy. He'd be learning to hunt and the older wolves would wrestle and fight with him, and teach him how to fit in with the pack. He would learn his place. His behaviour was just natural for a pup.

Quickly, she clicked on *Send*.

She put on her coat and shoes, and picked up her bag. 'Ready,' she called back to Mum. They left the flat and went down the three flights of stairs and outside.

It was beginning to rain. Sylvie pulled up her hood and Mum put up her umbrella and held it over them both. Mum walked so fast Sylvie had to run to keep up.

'Did we keep you awake, all that talking again last night?' Mum asked her. 'Dad and me?'

'Not really,' Sylvie said. 'What were you talking about? Were you arguing? Is it about the shop? Is Dad going to lose his job?'

'Oh Sylvie.' Mum stopped walking for a moment and looked directly at her. 'It's all going to be fine. Really. There are bound to be changes if the shop gets sold, but that might not happen. And Dad's full of good ideas. If we could borrow some money . . . ' Her voice tailed off. 'I don't want you worrying about it. Promise me? I know what you're like!'

How on earth could she promise that? 'Will you be home when I get back from school?' Sylvie asked instead.

'Not today. Parents' evening, remember? But you'll be OK for a little while, won't you? Dad will be back soon after five.'

They'd got to the corner where Sylvie turned off and Mum went straight on, to her school.

'Have a lovely day!' Mum kissed her. 'Why don't you ask Holly to come home with you after school?'

Sylvie nodded. 'Bye, Mum.'

Holly was hovering in the school foyer, waiting for her. Because it was a wet morning, everyone was allowed to go straight into the classroom and get on with reading or talking quietly. Holly and Sylvie hung their damp coats up on the pegs outside Class Six and went in.

'You OK?' Holly asked.

Sylvie nodded. She got her book out of her bag and put it on the table.

Holly scrabbled about in her own bag and brought out a stack of turquoise envelopes. 'Party invitations!' she said. She flipped through the pile till she found the one with Sylvie's name on the front, in gold letters, decorated with stars.

'Oh! You made up your mind, then?' Sylvie was a bit surprised. Holly had only been talking about it at the weekend, and they hadn't decided anything together. She opened the envelope.

Dear Sylvie

Please come to my birthday bonfire party
on November 12th

At 6 p.m.–9 p.m.

Love,
Holly

'There'll be food, and fireworks and a bonfire,'
Holly said. She was passing out invitations to other
people now. One of the envelopes said *Zak*, Sylvie
noticed. She didn't say anything.

Mrs Francis was getting her book out and settling
down to read. They always started the day like this,
before the register. The classroom was surprisingly
quiet. It was the nicest part of the day, Sylvie sometimes thought. She got her wolf book out of her bag
and began the next chapter. *How wolves communicate
with each other.*

Her mind began to drift . . .

A single wolf trotted through the trees, almost invisible in the dappled shade of the forest. Bushy tail low, back level, head down, he moved purposefully. Up, up he went. The higher he climbed, the more rocky it became. Trees thinning, then no trees: the bare rock of the mountain. He stopped, sniffed the air, ears pricked and alert.

He was less well camouflaged out in the bright sunlight. The greys and browns and gold of his fur showed up against white rock. A sound came in his throat, a high-pitched whimper, like a whistle, almost: a clear, carrying sound. Was he calling for another wolf?

'Sylvie?'

'*Si?*' She spoke Italian, without thinking, suddenly startled by hearing her name.

A giggle went round the class.

Sylvie blushed.

Mrs Francis was smiling at her. 'You were lost in your book, obviously! But we're doing the register now, Sylvie. Please put the book away.'

Holly nudged her. 'You were miles away!'

'I was thinking about wolves,' Sylvie whispered. 'One wolf, in particular.'

'Well stop! You're getting silly about them, now. You never think about anything else!'

Mrs Francis frowned. 'Sshh, you two.'

Sylvie felt hot. She hated being the centre of attention, or being in trouble. She was quiet for the rest of the morning.

At dinner time, Sylvie went to fetch her lunch box from the trolley. Holly was already sitting down with a group of Year Six kids. One of them was Zak. She hadn't saved a seat for Sylvie. She didn't even notice Sylvie, hovering in the doorway to the hall.

Sylvie sat down at another table. She ate her sandwiches quickly, without talking. Every so often she looked up at Holly, but she was laughing, or busy chatting away with the girls next to her. They would all be coming to the party, Sylvie realized.

Sylvie left the dining hall and went back to the classroom by herself.

Mrs Francis was cutting up paper. She looked up. 'Oh good! I could do with some help. Would you mind, Sylvie?'

Sylvie spent the rest of the lunch hour cutting green paper into the shapes of leaves for the reading tree on the classroom wall.

At the end of the day, Sylvie walked with Holly out of school. Holly didn't seem to have noticed how quiet Sylvie had been all day. She chatted on as normal. She was excited about the party. Zak said he would come, and she'd invited his friend Ahmed, too.

They got to the corner of the road where Holly turned off.

'See you tomorrow! Bye, Sylvie!'

'Bye,' Sylvie said. She watched Holly walking away. She didn't turn back or wave or anything.

It was silly, getting upset so easily. Sylvie knew that, really. Of course it was fine for Holly to have a party, and lots of other friends. And maybe Holly was right: she *was* getting a bit boring, talking about Star so much, always worrying about things.

She walked slowly past the shops, crossed the busy main road at the lights, went down the avenue and across the road to the terraced houses, and finally cut through to the flats. The rain had stopped, but there were big puddles all over the tarmac: pools of silver sky. The air smelt of car fumes and fried food. Someone was playing music: a violin that made a sad sound. As she went up the first lot of stairs, she remembered that Mum was going to be late back. Too late to ask Holly round, now. She rummaged in her bag for her key. The key-ring had a picture on it: a little photo of Bella, her mouth open as if she was smiling. Sylvie felt her eyes prickle with tears.

She changed into jeans and a T-shirt. The flat was hot: the central heating was on. She poured herself a glass of orange and mango juice and took it into the living room. She switched on the computer and waited for it to whirr into life. It was old, and took ages to do anything.

She logged on. Yes! A new message from Nonna.

Gramps and I are sorry you won't be visiting us
this autumn but Christmas will come round soon
enough, and it will be good for your mum and dad to
save the money. We are busy here with the garden
and bees. I have been making jam. We have had
big storms: your Star does not like the thunder.
Bella and he spent the night under the table on
the verandah! He is sweet but a little too wild and
bouncy. Gramps is trying to teach him to sit and
walk to heel but he is not learning very fast.
Vince says it is a waste of time as he is too much
wild wolf and we will make trouble for ourselves.
How is school? And your friend Holly?
Work hard and have some fun too.
All our love.
Ciao, Nonna and Gramps.

Sylvie felt suddenly furious. Why hadn't Mum said
they wouldn't be going to Nonna's at half-term? They
always went. And it was more important than ever,
now she had to train Star. He would have forgotten
her completely by Christmas. What was the point of
pretending Star was her puppy, when she was never
there?

She read the bit about Uncle Vince again. That made her cross too.

The phone rang. Sylvie picked it up.

'Hi, darling. You OK?' Dad's voice. 'I'm just leaving the shop now. Be with you in half an hour. OK?'

'No! I'm not OK,' Sylvie said in her crossest voice. 'Why didn't you tell me? That we're not going to Italy at half term. Nonna's just said . . . '

'Oh, Sylvie!' Dad said. 'I'm sorry we didn't tell you first. But we're saving money. You know we need to do that.'

Sylvie couldn't speak.

'I know you're disappointed,' Dad said. 'We can talk about it when I get home. I won't be long now. Think what you'd like for supper. Have a look in the freezer.'

Sylvie put back the phone.

She went to get her school bag. As she fished out the wolf book, the party invitation fell out onto the floor. She thought about Holly.

Nothing was going right today.

She switched on the telly. It was a load of rubbish, but it meant she didn't have to think about Holly or Nonna or Star any more. Not for a little while, at least.

Chapter 16

❦

November 12th

Sylvie stood in front of the full-length mirror in Mum and Dad's room. She pulled her hair back and up with both hands to see what that looked like. She let it go again, and it tumbled back over her shoulders. Anyway, what did it matter? They'd be outside in the dark, wouldn't they? And she knew everyone there, and it wasn't as if she'd got to impress anyone.

Mum drove her to Holly's house. 'I'll collect you at nine o'clock,' she said. She leaned over and kissed Sylvie. 'Be careful of the fireworks, won't you?'

'Of course!' Sylvie was still sitting in the car. Not nervous exactly, but . . .

'Off you go then! Have fun! Say happy birthday to Holly from me.'

Sylvie climbed out of the car seat, shut the door and walked slowly up the steps to Holly's front door.

Holly opened it immediately, as if she'd been waiting at the window for Sylvie to arrive. 'At last!' she said. She hugged Sylvie tight. 'It's not properly my birthday till you get here!'

Sylvie felt happiness bubble through her, like the fizz on lemonade.

She was still Holly's best friend.

'This is for you.' She handed Holly a parcel in shiny turquoise paper with silver ribbon.

Holly tore it open straightaway. 'Thanks Sylvie. It's really pretty.'

'It's for writing and drawing and anything you want, really,' Sylvie said. 'I've got one, but yours is prettier.'

Holly smoothed her hand over the cover of the notebook. Gold and copper coloured flowers on a black background. The pages inside were smooth and creamy.

'The bonfire's already alight.' Holly jiggled from one foot to another. 'Everyone's here now. Come on. Let's go into the garden.'

Sylvie forgot about being shy, even though there were lots of people: Holly's parents' friends, as well as people from her class. Zak and Ahmed were poking sticks at the fire, to make sparks fly up into the sky. Mia, Suna, and Lily were writing their names in the air with sparklers. Holly's mum lit a sparkler for Sylvie to hold. 'Put gloves on first,' she said. 'They are white hot, remember, even when they go out. Put the finished ones in the bucket of water.'

Happy Birthday Holly! Sylvie wrote with her sparkler, leaving red trails in the air. She drew three kisses.

'OK. Keep well back, everyone. We're about to light the fireworks!' Holly's dad drew an imaginary line with his foot to show them where to stand behind.

The first rocket whooshed into the sky. It exploded into stars. Sylvie watched the stars tumble back down to earth, leaving wisps of smoke against the night sky. The next rocket shot up, and another. A Catherine wheel spun and spattered from the tree. The garden filled up with the thick coloured smoke left behind by roman candles and traffic lights and fireworks with other funny names. Sylvie kept her hands over her ears. The bangs seemed extra loud in the walled city garden. Somewhere far off, a dog barked and a siren screamed.

When all the fireworks were finished, they piled more wood on the fire. They watched the flames leap and dance. Holly's mum brought out food: sausages and baked potatoes and salads, and then trays of sticky toffee and brownies. Last of all was the birthday cake, with eleven candles. The candles wouldn't stay alight for more than a second: they all had to crowd round, to

make a wind break, so Holly could light them again and blow them out. They sang 'Happy Birthday' and her eyes shone in the light from the flickering fire.

The fire began to go down. It was cold; the sky clear and peppered with stars. People began to drift back into the house. Finally it was just Holly, Sylvie, Zak, and Ahmed standing round the glowing embers of the bonfire. No one said much. It was just nice, being there. Zak and Ahmed seemed different, out of school, Sylvie realized. Not so silly. Perhaps they all were different: her too. Perhaps school didn't bring out the best in people.

Holly reached out and squeezed her hand. 'OK?' she whispered.

Sylvie nodded. 'It's beautiful, isn't it?'

The moon was rising: a silver half moon, glittery in the cold air.

'Time to go back in,' Holly said, shivering.

'How was it?' Mum asked as she drove Sylvie home afterwards.

'Magical,' Sylvie said. 'A bonfire party's a really good idea for a birthday.'

'You could have one, when it's yours,' Mum said. She slowed down for the traffic lights ahead.

'How? We haven't got a garden!'

'No, but maybe at Nonna's?'

'But how could I have any friends come to that? Honestly, Mum!'

Sylvie was quiet for the last bit of the journey.

134

Sylvie was in bed, reading. Mum came in with a pile of clean clothes and put them on the chair. 'It's very late,' Mum said. 'You should have your light out by now.' She came over and sat on the end of the bed. She hadn't done that for ages.

Sylvie stopped reading. She closed the book, put it on the bedside table and waited for Mum to say something.

'I'm sorry about not going to Italy at half-term,' Mum finally said. 'I know you were really disappointed.'

'What's the point of letting me have a puppy I never see?' Sylvie swallowed back sobs that seemed to well up from nowhere the minute she thought about Star.

'I know it's hard,' Mum said. 'Dad and I are trying to sort out our money situation. And that means cutting back a bit on things. Like flights to Italy. If we could borrow a lot of money from the bank, we might be able to buy the bookshop, instead of renting it, and then we could move into the flat at the top. And if we owned the whole house, then we'd own the little garden at the back, too. But it still won't be big enough for Star, I'm afraid.'

'So what's the point?' Sylvie wriggled down under

the duvet and turned over, so Mum couldn't see her face.

Mum reached out her hand, as if to stroke Sylvie's head, but she ducked away under the duvet.

'We'll still be seeing Nonna and Gramps at Christmas,' Mum said. 'And Bella and Star.'

'I'm too tired to talk,' Sylvie said. 'Can you go away now?'

Mum sighed. But she stood up and turned out Sylvie's light and went out of the room.

Sylvie listened to the sound of her footsteps going down the hall and into the kitchen, and then Dad's voice, saying something to Mum.

She was tired. Sleepy. She let her mind drift off. She dreamed she was at Nonna's house, and Bella and Star were walking either side of her, up the steep track through the forest, their paws padding silently on the soft earth.

Somewhere, a wolf howled, and another answered.

The sound made goosepimples prickle up the skin on her arms.

It was a whole month and a bit till she could see Star again. She started counting the days.

Chapter 17

❧

December: Italy

Rain fell in great slanting sheets, so that from
Gramps's van Sylvie could see only the blurred
shadows of the mountains cloaked in mist and cloud.
The river Serchio was high, almost at the top of the
banks, rushing and tumbling down the valley, totally
different from in summer when it moved sluggishly
in the heat, a ribbon of green winding between the
banks. Today the water was a muddy, swirling brown;
whole trees were being carried down on the fast
current, catching at the bridge supports.

It was too wet to get out of the van; Gramps, Mum
and Dad drank coffee from a flask that Nonna had

packed into a basket for the journey back from the airport, together with mozzarella and tomato sandwiches made with slabs of home-made bread. For Sylvie, there was a separate flask with hot chocolate. She sipped slowly from the cup, warming her hands round it.

'This rain will turn to snow when night falls,' Gramps said. 'In the mountains, at least. So you might get your white Christmas, Sylvie.'

'Good,' Sylvie said. 'I hope it snows so much we get snowed in and then we'll have to stay all winter.' She took a big bite of sandwich. The journey seemed to have taken for ever. They'd waited ages at the airport in London, and then Gramps had to drive really slowly from Pisa to Lucca because of the wet roads.

'We should get going again,' Gramps said. 'Drink up. Nonna will be wondering what's keeping us.'

'Star's never seen snow,' Sylvie said. 'I wonder what he'll do.'

Gramps laughed. 'Same as usual, I reckon. Run like a mad thing and bark and make a right kerfuffle. He's taken to howling some nights, and once or twice we've heard the wolves howling back. The bad weather brings them down from the mountains, closer to home.'

'Oh dear,' Mum said. 'That's not so good, is it?'

Gramps didn't answer. He was concentrating hard on driving. The roads were steeper and narrower now, climbing all the way.

'Sit still, Sylvie!' Dad said. 'You're wriggling around like a cat on hot bricks!'

'I'm excited!' Sylvie said. 'It's taking too long to get there.'

'Star will be in the barn when we arrive,' Gramps said. 'He's not very safe around cars and people. He'll need to take it slowly, get used to you. Don't expect too much straight away, Sylvie.'

'Won't he remember me at all?' she asked anxiously. 'All that time I spent with him when he was so little?'

'We'll have to wait and see,' Gramps said. 'Who knows what animals remember?'

Over and over, Sylvie had tried to imagine what it would be like, arriving at the farm. In her best imaginings, Star recognized her instantly; there would be a special bond between them that everyone would see. He would run up to her, and whimper and yip with joy. He'd lick her hand and sit close to her, and because he trusted her he'd be easy to train. She'd teach him to sit and stay and come when called. He'd learn to walk by her side. Nonna and Gramps would be amazed.

She must have dozed off. It was already dark, and the van had stopped in front of the house. Nonna was standing at the open door, and Bella was wagging her tail and barking.

The moment she stepped out of the van Sylvie heard the yip-yipping sound coming from the barn. It was still raining. The air was colder than ever.

'Come inside, quick!' Nonna called.

Sylvie ran into the shelter of the porch. 'Hello Nonna!' She gave her a big hug. 'I can hear Star! Can I see him now? Please please please?'

'You've hardly arrived! Let's get the bags in and have a cup of tea and then we'll go out to the barn together, if you like. You can take him his dinner.'

Everything seemed to take ages. Sylvie danced from foot to foot as the adults chatted and carried bags upstairs, drank tea and ate cake. 'Hurry up!' she said to Nonna.

Mum shushed her. 'Don't be so rude, Sylvie!'

But at last Nonna was ready, putting on her coat and boots. She showed Sylvie the bag of dry dog food in the larder, and she took a bowl of chicken meat out of the fridge. 'You carry all that,' she said, 'and I'll hold the umbrella.'

Already, the rain was turning to sleet. Sylvie and Nonna shivered and pulled up their hoods. Together they crossed the garden to the barn, behind the shed where Star had been born and where Bella slept on cold nights. Star had heard them: he was whimpering, and scratching the door.

Nonna unlatched and slowly opened the barn door. 'Keep back,' she said to Sylvie, 'in case he jumps up. He gets very excited. He's strong, now.'

Sylvie saw his black nose and grey muzzle, first, and the big sandy coloured paws, and then there he was, all of him: Star, who was supposed to be *her* pup, but who looked nothing like the small furry puppy she'd last seen in early September. She'd seen the photos of Star that Nonna had sent, of course, but even so . . . it was a shock to see him for real. He was as tall as Bella, with long slim legs, and pointed ears, a thick ruff of fur round his neck, and his tail, thick and furry, gold tipped with black, wagging wildly as he greeted Nonna. He whined and yipped and yelped. He didn't seem to see Sylvie at all for a few seconds, but then he stopped, and he stared, and the fur along his spine bristled and he made a soft sound in his throat.

'It's me, Star,' Sylvie said quietly.

Nonna held Star's collar while Sylvie put the dry dog food in one metal bowl and the chicken pieces in the other. He strained at the collar, so strong that he could pull Nonna right over if he wanted to, Sylvie realized. As soon as Nonna let go, Star lunged forwards. He crunched up the meat and he swallowed the lot. He wagged his tail as he licked the bowl clean and started on the dry food.

Sylvie watched him. Her eyes adjusted to the dim light. He'd finished the food already. He snuffled the empty bowls along the floor. He came sniffing round Nonna and Sylvie to look for more. For a second, she almost felt afraid.

'He's so like a wolf!' Sylvie whispered.

'Stroke him,' Nonna said. 'He's full of energy but he's soft-hearted too. He's Bella's puppy as much as he's wolf. Half and half, remember.'

Sylvie stretched out her hand and smoothed his back. The fur was thick and soft. *Winter pelage,* she remembered from the wolf book at home. Star sat down, and she stroked his head. He seemed to like it.

She rubbed his neck, and he shifted so he was leaning against her legs, a warm, heavy weight.

'He calms down when his stomach's full,' Nonna said. 'He's taken to you all right. Perhaps he remembers your smell. Or perhaps you smell like me and Gramps, so he knows instinctively you are part of the family.'

'Can I take him for a walk, tomorrow?'

'Yes, but not by yourself. Not till you've got used to each other properly.'

Star settled himself down on the straw. He lay on his side, legs outstretched, tail like a soft brush, gently wagging against the floor when either Nonna or Sylvie spoke. His mouth curved in a smile. Sylvie and Nonna sat down too, side-by-side on one of the bales stacked by the wall. It was almost warm, out of the wind, with the sweet smell of the straw and the musky smell of dog. Sylvie felt relief flood through her. He was the most beautiful dog she'd ever seen, and he belonged to her.

She thought about that later, lying in bed. *Belonged* wasn't the right word for it. Even she could see that. Star belonged to himself. He was half wild; he couldn't be owned by her or anyone else. Not really.

Wind rattled the wooden window shutters. Sylvie snuggled down deeper under the duvet. Perhaps right now the sleet was turning to softer, downy flakes of snow. If she wished hard enough . . .

Chapter 18

✦

She woke early. It was still dark, although the little clock on her bedside table said it was 7.55 a.m. Her nose was cold: there was no heating in the bedrooms at Nonna's. Sylvie wrapped the bedspread round her and went to the windows. She had to open them to get to the shutters, and the air whipped in.

She pushed back the shutters. The sky was grey, turning peach and blue at the eastern edge of the mountains, and everything—garden, road, barn roof, fields and mountains—was white with snow.

Yes! Her wish had worked.

Sylvie fastened the shutters back to let in the light and closed the window again. She got dressed as quickly as possible: socks, pants, leggings, trousers, vest, T-shirt and the thick jumper Nonna had knitted for her in beautiful flecked blue wool, the colour of sky mixed with bits of cornfield and wild meadow flowers.

Nonna was up already, cooking breakfast in the kitchen. '*Salve*, Sylvie!'

'It's snowed, Nonna! Can we take Star and Bella out in it?'

'Later, yes. You want to feed them by yourself this morning?'

'Yes!'

'Let Bella out of the shed first, for a wee, and then feed her before you go to Star in the barn. OK?'

'Doesn't he need to go out too?'

'Yes, before he has his food. He'll come back for that no problem. Then he must stay in the barn, but Bella can go where she wants, yes? Though she'll be trying to get in front of the fire all day!'

Sylvie pulled on her boots and took her thick coat from the hook in the hall. She opened the door and stood for a moment in the porch, looking out over the snow-covered vine and the flower pots each with a thick white layer of icing. The sun was coming up, casting pink and blue shadows over the snowy garden. Birds had left their neat prints in the top layer of snow, and there were other marks: the prints of some small animal, drips from the trees.

Sylvie trod carefully, watching the trail her own feet left in the snow, and then she forgot to be careful and ran and jumped and made patterns all over the garden. Bella and Star barked and yipped. She opened the shed, first, and Bella shot out, ran in circles, biting at the snow. Sylvie put a handful of biscuits in her bowl and checked there was enough water in the other bowl. Bella wagged and bounced and trotted back to gulp down her breakfast.

'Coming, Star!' Sylvie called out, and her voice seemed to carry further in the cold air.

Star whined and scratched at the barn door. The moment she unlatched it, he shot out, but he skidded to a halt as he felt the wet snow on his paws for the first time.

Sylvie laughed. 'It's only snow,' she told him. He sniffed it and bit at it, and then he too ran and

rolled and dug at it with his paws. He chased Bella and they ran together, playing.

Her hands were already freezing. She poured the biscuits into the bowl and put the pieces of meat in the other. She went to the outside tap to get more water but it was frozen solid. She fetched some from the kitchen; by the time she got back Star was wolfing down the dog biscuits and polishing the bowls with his pink tongue. He barked at her. *More!* he seemed to be saying. *Hungry! Feed me!*

Sylvie closed the barn door and sat down on the straw bales. Star sat too, his head cocked to one side, as if he was puzzled. He watched her, ears pricked forwards.

Sylvie talked to him softly, keeping her voice calm and level. 'Good boy, Star. We'll go out together soon. My beautiful dog.'

A tractor rumbled slowly and noisily up the road.

Star narrowed his eyes. His ears went back.

'It's OK,' she told him. 'Nothing's going to hurt you.'

Star stood up, he came up and sniffed her feet. She stayed still, letting him sniff her boots and her coat. She kept her hands in her lap, so he wouldn't feel threatened.

The noise faded into the distance. Star settled down. He looked at her again, and whined softly.

'What do you want, Star?' she asked.

He pricked up his ears as if he was listening to her. He got up, walked over and whined at the barn door.

'You want to go out. Shall we play outside? Is that what you'd like?'

He looked at her again, eyes bright. He dashed between her and the door, yipping with excitement as she got up and opened the door.

He tumbled outside, and she ran after him across the snowy garden. She threw snowballs for him to chase, and he bounced and bounded after them, confused when they turned to mush.

Bella trotted across the snowy lawn. Star greeted her, nuzzling her and making soft sounds of pleasure in his throat. They ran together, chasing and mock fighting. Bella was still the one in charge, Sylvie noticed, even though Star was as tall as her now.

'Doesn't that look fun!' Dad had come out to watch them playing in the snow. 'Nonna says come and have some breakfast.'

'Can't we take them for a walk first? Please please please, Dad. The snow's so beautiful and it's already beginning to melt.'

'Just a short one, then. I'll go and tell Nonna and Gramps that's what we're doing.'

'Come, Bella. Come, Star!'

Bella came at once. Star kept playing, but as soon as Sylvie started walking away with Bella he bounded after them. Dad clipped the leather lead to his collar.

'Does he have to go on that?'

'Yes. Gramps is very clear: Star's to stay on the lead the whole time. We don't want him running off any-where near Vince's farm and causing merry havoc.'

The snow was already turning to slush on the track, churned into muddy brown tyre-prints where a tractor had gone up the hill to Vince's farm. But as they walked higher, up over the meadow, the snow was still white and frozen, and the branches of the chestnut and beech trees when they reached the edge of the forest were iced white. Up here, snow muffled the usual sounds. Star and Bella walked quietly; even Star stopped pulling at the leash. He stopped every so often and lifted his head, as if he was tasting the air for scents that were camouflaged by the cold.

'Bet he's warm as toast in that fur coat,' Dad said. 'Pretty, isn't he?'

'He's the most beautiful dog I've ever seen,' Sylvie said. 'And he's being good as anything. Can't we just let him off the lead for a short while? We're nowhere near the farm now.'

'No,' Dad said. 'You heard what Gramps said.'

Sylvie sighed. It didn't seem fair. Star wouldn't go far from Bella, she was sure of that now.

'Have you ever seen the wolves in the mountains?' she asked Dad.

He shook his head. 'Never. Not even once.'

'I wish I could hear them howling. I bet that sounds amazing.'

They'd got to the place where the track forked, under a big sweet chestnut tree.

'I need my breakfast,' Dad said. 'We'll turn back, now.'

Bella understood. She started trotting back down the path. She knew exactly where it went, even though it was covered in snow.

'It must be amazing to be able to find your way like that,' Sylvie said.

Bella went much faster, downhill. Star pulled at the lead, choking and spluttering. Sylvie's arm ached from trying to rein him in. She let Dad hold him for a bit. 'We've got to train him to walk to heel,' she said. 'And to sit and stay and come when he's called. If he can learn all that, he'll be fine.'

'You know all about it, don't you?' Dad said. He smiled at her. 'All those books you've been reading.'

'Yes.'

She took the lead back from Dad, even though her arm still hurt. She jerked back the lead. 'Heel, Star!' she said each time. But it didn't seem to make any difference. He pulled and strained all the way home.

Christmas in Italy was different from Christmas in London. Or perhaps the difference was simply that here they were deep in the countryside, a long way from shops and people. They opened presents on Christmas Eve, in front of the fire. They didn't watch television, but one of Nonna's presents from Mum was a DVD and they watched it together after supper. Bella and Star were both allowed in the house for a short while, to lie in front of the wood-burning stove, until the stink of hot wet dog got too strong, and Nonna shooed them both back out to the barn and the shed.

They had to drag Star by his collar to make him go. He yipped and whined and scratched at the barn door the moment Dad closed it. They could still hear him crying when they got back inside the house.

'Can't he stay inside the house, just tonight?' Sylvie begged. 'It is Christmas, Nonna! It's so cold outside.'

Nonna was firm. 'No, Sylvie. He's not a house dog. He's too big, too wild, and too noisy. No one will get a wink of sleep. And he has the thickest fur coat, remember; he's designed for the cold!'

Sylvie woke with a start in the middle of the night. Was that Star she could hear, howling from the barn? Or a lone wolf, who had made her way down from the mountains, calling for her pack? The sound sent shivers down Sylvie's spine. But it was exciting, too. The eerie wildness of it, like something calling from another world. It was like nothing she had ever heard before.

Chapter 19

At Aunty Maria and Uncle Vince's house the next day for Christmas lunch, the adults were talking about the wolves. Everyone had heard the howling in the night. Sylvie listened quietly.

Uncle Vince was furious. He said he'd get a gun out and shoot the wolves if they came anywhere near his farm. He might get some special poison too, to kill them.

'They should put a stop to it right now,' Uncle Vince said. He banged his spoon on the table and made the plates and glasses rattle. 'Ridiculous, to make wolves a protected species in this day and age.

What nonsense! Shows how out of touch the politicians are with the real farmers. They know nothing, these city people, with their villas in Rome.'

Sylvie's cousin Tomas spoke up. 'Well, they have a special feeling about wolves, of course, in Rome. That story about the founding of the city: Romulus and Remus were brought up by wolves. Remember that story, Sylvie?'

She nodded. She did, sort of.

'Don't get so worked up!' Nonna was saying to Uncle Vince. 'The wolves stay in the mountains most of the time.'

'Not when the lambs are born,' Uncle Vince said. 'And especially not if the snow comes thick again like last winter.'

'Nonna told us about the wolf-dog pup,' Tomas said to Sylvie.

Uncle Vince scowled across the table. 'Don't get me started! That's just asking for trouble, keeping a dog that's half wolf. Should have got rid of it at birth!'

Tears came in Sylvie's eyes. And then she was suddenly angry, too. He'd no right to talk like that!

Nonna must have seen her expression. She reached out for Sylvie's hand and squeezed it. Skilfully she changed the subject. 'Now, it's Christmas everyone. Let us enjoy this wonderful food that Maria has prepared for us, and show some respect for her cooking. No more angry words.'

Gramps poured wine for the grown-ups. That meant everyone except Sylvie: Tomas and Sebastian counted as grown-ups now. 'We raise our glasses for a toast! Salut!'

Sylvie held up her glass of peach juice. Everyone cheered, and clinked glasses. Gramps bowed his head and said the grace: *thank you for family, and good food, and fellowship.* Nonna, Aunty Maria, Mum and Dad said *Amen* very loudly.

Aunty Maria served the roast goose, and Mum and Nonna passed the vegetables round. It was funny, the way the women always did the food, Sylvie thought. Old-fashioned. She imagined what Holly would say.

It was two years since Sylvie had last seen Tomas and Seb, and they seemed much nicer than she remembered. After lunch, they went into the living room in front of the fire, and played games with her: card games, and draughts, and then they taught her how to play chess. They let her win. Tomas said he would like to see Star. He promised to go for a walk with Sylvie and Star before he went back to the city. He told her about his girlfriend, Micheala. She was going to be a lawyer one day, like him.

'What do you want to be, Sylvie, when you grow up?' he asked her.

'I don't know,' Sylvie said. 'A vet, maybe? Mainly I want to live somewhere where I can have a dog of my own.'

'You should come and live here in Italy, near us,' Tomas said. 'You are half Italian, after all.'

'Like Star!' Seb laughed. 'Half and half.'

Sylvie frowned. She didn't want to be *half* any-thing. She was just whole her. Sylvie. And Star was just Star.

The grown-ups were still talking and laughing round the table in the big kitchen. Sylvie thought how happy they all sounded. Gramps was proposing another toast, to celebrate.

'Celebrate what?' Sylvie called out. She went to the doorway. Mum and Dad looked flushed with happi-ness about something. Mum's eyes were shiny with tears, but she was smiling so much that Sylvie knew they were happy tears not sad ones.

Dad explained. 'Nonna and Gramps, Maria and Vince have done something truly marvellous. They have decided to help us by lending us some money. And that means we can raise enough to get a mortgage on the bookshop, Sylvie. We can move into the flat at the top. It will all be ours. Well, ours and the bank's—and Nonna, Gramps, Vince and Maria will all own a bit too!'

Sylvie squealed. She ran and hugged Nonna tight. It was the best Christmas present ever, to see Mum and Dad so happy. They would leave the flat on the estate, and instead she would be living just across the park from Holly. Now all she had to do was persuade Mum and Dad that the little garden was just big enough for a dog. That she could take Star for walks every single day in the park. Then all her dreams could come true at last.

'Can I go on your computer?' she asked Aunty Maria.

'What now? Today? At Christmas?' Aunty Maria looked shocked.

Sylvie laughed. 'Yes! I want to tell Holly about the bookshop straight away.'

Sylvie's fingers flew across the keyboard, typing out her message.

> Merry Christmas, Holly! Hope you are having
> fun and lovely presents. Best news ever: we are
> going to buy the bookshop building and live there
> too! WE will almost be neighbours!!! It has a
> garden. Tiny, but garden = room for a dog,
> yes?
> 😊 Sylvie xxxxxxx

She pressed send. Her heart was dancing.

Cousin Seb lent over her shoulder. 'Got a boy-friend, Sylvie?'

'NO!' Sylvie said indignantly. 'Holly is my best friend.'

Seb laughed. 'Just teasing you!'

'Well don't!'

It was supposed to be a joke, but it still made Sylvie squirm. It wasn't funny.

She went to the window and peered out. It was already getting dark. Star would be getting restless. He'd only had one walk, early this morning. He'd been cooped up in the barn all day.

She went to find Dad. 'Can we take Star out, for a quick walk?' she asked.

He shook his head. 'Not right now, Sylvie. We're still all enjoying our Christmas day here. Later, perhaps.'

Now she'd started thinking about Star, all she wanted to do was get back to him. The rest of the afternoon dragged on and on. The grown-ups were all being boring, just talking, and washing up, and dozing in their chairs in front of the wood-burner. Even Aunty Maria's dog was sleeping, curled up on her lap. Tomas and Seb had disappeared upstairs.

'I'm going back,' Sylvie announced. 'I need to let Star out for a run around, and give him his tea.'

Mum looked up. 'All right, love. Be careful, won't you, all by yourself? I'll come along in a little while, to make sure you're all right.'

'I'm nearly eleven, Mum!' Sylvie said. 'Of course I'll be all right.'

She closed the door behind her. It took a little while for her eyes to adjust in the dark. It was cold; the wind was blowing clouds across the sky. The first star was out. Sylvie shivered and wrapped her scarf round tighter. She wished she'd brought a torch. Everything looked different in the dark, even though she'd walked along the track hundreds of times before. The wind made the trees sigh and creak and cast deeper shadows. There was no one around, no cars going along the road down in the valley, even. Not a single light.

Now she could make out the dark shape of Nonna's house, and suddenly there was Bella! Wagging her tail, and making greeting noises in her throat as she came up the track towards Sylvie.

Sylvie hugged her, and rubbed her furry neck and smoothed her along her back. 'Sweet, good, darling Bella!' Now she felt totally safe. They walked together to the house, and Sylvie opened the front door and turned on all the lights. Bella plodded behind, keeping her company.

Sylvie collected up the dog food from the kitchen and went back out to the barn. Bella followed. Star had heard them. He was making his funny yip-yipping noise, and scratching at the bottom of the door. Sylvie opened it carefully, and he pushed and shoved at it, scrabbling to get out. He didn't greet her like Bella had, he was too desperate to get out.

He ran in circles round the garden, chasing his tail and tumbling over his big paws. He tried to make Bella play too: he nipped her tail and nuzzled her face and whimpered at her till she ran with him for a while, as if she were just tolerating him and being a good mum, paying him the attention he needed. He barked at the hens who had come out of the hen house to see what all the noise was about. These days, the hens had to live in a big wire pen Gramps had made to keep them safe from Star. In winter they wouldn't mind much, Sylvie thought. But in summer, it would be sad to see them caged up like that. She sighed. It wasn't simple, having Star here. It would be much better for Nonna and Gramps when he came to live with her, at the bookshop.

She tried not to think about what it might be like for Star. The upstairs flat, and the square of walled garden. But the park was only a short distance away, and there was lots of space there for a dog to run. It wasn't a wild place like the fields and forests and mountains, though. Nothing like.

She pushed open the barn door again and filled the food bowls for Star. He rushed in and swallowed down the meat and biscuits in big hungry bites. He looked around for more. He licked Sylvie's hands and then he jumped up to lick her face. He was heavy, and strong: she staggered back. 'Get down!' she said in her sternest voice. She had to show him she was the boss.

For a second he did sit down. He stared at her with his big golden eyes, and his mouth seemed to be smiling at her.

'Good dog, Star,' she told him. She wished she could let him come back into the house with her, but Nonna would be cross if he made a mess. So she left him in the barn, quickly closing the door behind her. His cries and whimpers followed her back to the house.

Bella trotted calmly back to the porch with her and flumped down. Her ears pricked as she listened to Star's cries. Finally he was quiet.

Sylvie couldn't settle. It wasn't right, leaving Star alone for such a long time. It wasn't good for him. But she couldn't think what else to do when Nonna and Gramps were being so strict.

She'd got her dog, sort of, but she hadn't expected it to feel like this. She didn't *really* have him.

She turned on the telly but the film was a boring old cowboy one and she soon lost interest.

How long till Mum came to check on her, she wondered? Or should she go back to Uncle Vince's farm? The thought of the cold, dark walk put her off. In the end, she put some more wood in the stove and read one of her new books from Dad in the warm. Even that didn't feel right. So she let Bella in to keep her company.

Bella lay quietly in front of the fire as if she was in heaven. She twitched her ears, as if she was listening out even while she dozed.

Soon enough Sylvie heard voices, and footsteps: Nonna, Gramps, Mum, and Dad were here at last.

'What's Bella doing inside?' Nonna asked.

'She's keeping me company,' Sylvie said. 'I was lonely by myself.'

'Oh darling!' Nonna put her arms round Sylvie and hugged her tight. 'We weren't so very long, were we?'

'It seemed ages,' Sylvie said. 'It's dark and cold and Star's lonely too, all by himself in the barn. It's not fair. It's not good for him.'

Nonna looked across at Gramps. Mum was watching them both too.

Nonna sighed. 'Well, all right; Star can come by the fire for just a little while this evening, as long as he can stay calm and quiet. But we mustn't make a habit of it. He isn't a house dog, Sylvie, and he never will be. You have got to understand that.'

Sylvie nodded. 'I know, Nonna. Thank you.'

Mum went with her to get Star. The garden was dark and icy. The hens clucked softly from their hen house as they walked past. They would be tucked up side by side on the perch, their feathers fluffed out, keeping each other warm.

The moment Sylvie opened the barn door Star bounded out across the garden, chasing shadows and yipping with joy. Sylvie called him to her, and he ran up, tail wagging. She held onto his collar.

'See? He does know his name,' Sylvie said. 'He is learning things.'

Mum was quiet.

'Now come quietly, Star!' Sylvie kept hold of his collar and walked him round the side of the house, through the door into the hall. She opened the sitting room door.

Bella sat up, ears pricked. Star pulled away from Sylvie; he ran over to Bella and licked her face and made soft whimpering sounds in his throat. Bella and Star lay down side by side in front of the fire.

'See?' Sylvie said. 'He's happy now. That's all he wanted.'

Gramps opened his mouth to say something, but Nonna shushed him. 'It's Sylvie's Christmas treat,' she said. 'Tomorrow and the rest of the holiday, we'll go back to normal.'

'Thank you,' Sylvie said. For this moment, everything was perfect. She wouldn't think about the other nights, or having to leave him all over again when it was time to go back to London.

Chapter 20

❧

London: January/February

'How are you two getting on?' Mum put her head round the door. She laughed. 'You've both got orange highlights in your hair! Did you know?'

Sylvie stopped painting for a moment and looked at Holly. Mum was right: Holly had streaks of paint on her fringe and all down one side. 'Will it come off?' she asked.

'Yes, it's only water-based paint. It'll all come off in the shower.' Mum came further into Sylvie's bedroom. 'You're doing a great job. It's coming along beautifully. It positively glows in here, like a Tuscan villa in the sun.'

'What does *Tuscan* mean?' Holly asked.

'It's the bit of Italy where Nonna and Gramps live: Northern Tuscany,' Sylvie explained.

Her new bedroom was going to look amazing when it was finished. One dark red wall, one purple, and two in this orange colour. The paint tin called it *Burnt Umber.*

'It's hard work,' Holly said. 'My arm's aching like mad.'

'Coffee break for the workers, then?' Mum said. 'Or home-made lemonade, if you prefer? Put the lids on the paint pots and wrap the brushes in cling-film so they don't dry out.'

Sylvie stood at the kitchen window, at the back of the house. You could see the trees in the park from here: a big mass of bare branches that in spring and summer would be all different colour greens, beyond roof tops and chimneys and back yards. It was quieter this side of the house, away from the traffic along the High Street.

Holly came over and looked out too. 'It's quite small, isn't it?' She peered down. 'More like a back-yard than a garden, really.'

From up here, a bird's eye view, it did look tiny. A walled square of cracked concrete, with two dust-bins, a shrubby plant against one brick wall, and a few pots of dead sticks next to a rotting wooden shed.

'It's a mess!' Mum said. 'But when we've cleared away the shed and all the old rubbish, and planted bulbs and flowers in the pots, and sorted it out, it will be nice. We can have a table and chairs out there, for eating outside on sunny days.'

'You could have a guinea pig hutch,' Holly said. 'Or even a cat.'

Sylvie knew she'd never have a guinea pig in a cage. She didn't want a cat, either, really. But even she knew that the garden was not big enough for a tiny dog, let alone one who was half wolf. Sadly she turned away from the window and sat down at the table to drink her lemonade.

Mum placed a jug of daffo-dils in the middle of the table. 'A touch of early spring,' she said. 'I bought them in the supermarket. But next year perhaps we'll grow some of our own.'

'When do you think you'll be moving in properly?' Holly asked.

'As soon as we've finished decorating, and sorted out the boiler, and put the new bathroom in,' Mum said. 'Late March or early April. The beginning of the Easter holidays, perhaps.'

'It's so exciting!' Holly said. She was still at the window, standing on tip-toe and craning her neck to see as far as she could. 'You can almost see the top of my house from here! That's the church at the end of my road, I think. How cool is that, Sylvie?'

'It's the best thing of all,' Sylvie said.

'OK, back to work!' Mum said, finishing her coffee. 'Let's all do another hour of painting and then I'll take you both for some lunch at the corner café.'

Being shut in the barn too much was making Star cross and badly behaved, Nonna told Sylvie on Skype. Sylvie had been right about that. So, now that the weather was getting better and she and Gramps were busy working on the garden, planting seeds in the cold frames and pruning the fruit trees, they'd started letting him roam round the garden like Bella. He was slowly learning not to bark so much, and sometimes he would come when they called him. It was progress of a *limited* kind. They left him tied on a long lead when they went out, and shut him in the barn at night. It was a good *compromise*, Nonna said.

'Is he happier now?' Sylvie asked.

'Yes, I think so.' But Nonna sighed, heavily.

She looked older tonight, Sylvie thought. Her face was more wrinkly. But it could just be the camera on Aunty Maria's new computer.

'How is the new flat coming along?' Nonna asked.

'Good! We hung new curtains at the weekend,' Sylvie said. 'My bedroom is finished. The builders have started on the bathroom.'

'And school?'

Sylvie frowned. 'Too many tests. And everyone is going on about which school they're going to in September.'

Nonna smiled. 'You and Holly will go together, yes?'

'I really hope so! As long as we both get a place there.'

Nonna tutted. 'It's a very strange thing, all these different schools. Why don't they have just one local school for all the children to go to, together?'

Sylvie didn't want to talk about school. 'Will you send me another photo of Star?' she asked. 'I'm going to pin all the photos of him from when he was born till now on a board in my new room.'

'I'll take some new ones and email you, and you print them out, yes?'

'Thanks Nonna.'

'Now I must go!' Nonna blew her a kiss. In the background, Sylvie could see Aunty Maria moving about; she waved at Sylvie as she went behind Nonna's chair. '*Ciao*, Sylvie.'

The screen went blank.

Sylvie sat there a little longer, thinking about Nonna and Gramps, Bella and Star. They suddenly seemed a very long way away.

Chapter 21

March

Sylvie sat at the computer in the living room, looking at a website about a project to keep wolves away from sheep in the Swiss Alps. The wolves were thought to have come into Switzerland from Italy. And the farmers were cross about the wolves killing lambs. But they'd come up with a solution. Instead of trying to kill the wolves, they were using traditional shepherd dogs and real life shepherds, like in olden times, to protect the sheep and keep them safe. The dogs were a special breed called *Maremma*, from Italy. Sylvie studied the photo of them: really big dogs with white fur, totally gorgeous. The puppies were brought up with lambs from when they were six or seven weeks old. They learned to be gentle with sheep, but fiercely protective of the flock.

All day at school she'd been worrying about the email Nonna had sent her.

> Yesterday Vince found two new-born lambs dead in
> the field, but not eaten, so probably not wild wolves.
> Vince thinks it was Star who killed them. He has
> been suspicious about Star before. And it is true
> that we left Star tied up when we went shopping in
> Lucca, and when we came back he had chewed
> through the rope, so he had been running free
> that morning.
> Oh Sylvie I am sorry to tell you this news.

Sylvie's tummy churned with worry. She knew, even though Nonna hadn't said it, that Uncle Vince's solution would be to get rid of Star. He'd been going on about it for months now, how Star was *a problem, an accident waiting to happen, a huge mistake.*

What if she could persuade him to get a Maremma to guard his lambs? She couldn't quite imagine Uncle Vince going back to the old farming traditions. And even if she did convince him, it couldn't happen soon enough to save Star. If her uncle actually saw Star near the sheep again, he would shoot him.

Sylvie's eyes filled with tears. There had to be another way, if only she could work it out. Perhaps they could find a home for Star with a family who had a big garden but no animals. And as he got older, he'd calm down, perhaps. Her head ached with the effort of thinking about it.

Only two days to go. By this time on Saturday she'd be in Italy, and she would see Star, and she could talk properly to Nonna and Gramps about what to do.

Mum called to her from the kitchen. 'Have you started packing up your things, Sylvie?'

'Not yet,' Sylvie said.

'What are you doing?'

'Just . . . stuff.' Sylvie sighed. She turned off the computer. She went into her bedroom. There was so much to pack. She started with the books.

Mum came to the doorway with a large black bin bag. 'Moving house is a golden opportunity to get rid of things you don't need,' she said. 'We don't want to be cluttering up the new flat with a lot of old junk. Think of it as a fresh start.' She went back to the kitchen. Delicious smells of tomatoes and herbs wafted through the flat.

Sylvie took the top shelf of books and stacked them neatly at the bottom of a cardboard box. She hesitated as she looked at the next shelf. *Wolves. How to Train your New Puppy. Dog Whispering for Beginners. Eye of the Wolf. A Dog so Small. Grimm's Selected Tales. The Snow Goose. Born to Run. The Enchanted Horse. Mog the Cat.* She put each one carefully into the cardboard box. She needed *all* her books, she decided: even the ones she'd had as a baby. They were part of who she was.

All evening, she carried on sorting her possessions into boxes. Clothes, toys, all the things she'd had since she was really little. She hardly threw anything away. It should have been exciting, getting ready to move at last, but she was too full of worry about Star.

After supper, Sylvie turned the computer back on and checked her messages. There was nothing new from Nonna. She flicked back to the site about conserving European wolves, and the Maremma. She wrote an email to Nonna, sending her the link.

Look at this, Nonna! About the old ways of protecting sheep from wolves. See you Saturday xxx

Nonna might tell Uncle Vince about it. If anyone could persuade him, it would be her.

'Stop messing about on that computer!' Dad said. 'We've still got packing and tidying to do, remember? The removal men are going to be here at nine tomorrow morning.'

'I've done my room,' Sylvie said. 'Everything except the bed clothes and I need them for sleeping in.'

The plan was for Sylvie to stay with Holly tomorrow after school, and then the next day Mum would take her to the airport and put her on the plane. For the first time ever, she was going to fly out to Italy by herself for the first bit of the holidays. Nonna and Gramps would be waiting for her at Pisa airport.

It was all easy enough; she'd done the journey so many times before. It would give Mum and Dad time to sort out the flat, and then Mum would come to join her for a few days and they would fly home together.

The flat looked strange, crowded with boxes. The removal men would pack up the furniture and the rest of the kitchen stuff. Sylvie checked the small bag of things she'd packed ready to take with her to Italy. She didn't need much: she had clothes and coats and boots at Nonna and Gramps's house already.

'Well,' Mum said, looking around. 'Will you be sad to leave this place?'

'Not really,' Sylvie said. 'Our new flat is a million times nicer.'

'We've been happy here, though, haven't we?'

'Of course we have!' Dad put his arms round Mum and slow-danced with her round the living room, steering her between the boxes. 'But you know the saying: one door shuts and another door opens! The next chapter of our lives is about to start. And I for one can't wait!'

Sylvie opened the window and leaned out. The sounds of the city floated up. Cars and sirens, a car alarm. Music from one of the other flats. The sky was lit up by the orange glow of street lights and the lights left on all night in office blocks and shops and houses. An aeroplane started its descent towards the airport, lights flashing into the dark. A flock of pigeons flew in one big curve, so close she could hear the beat of their wings.

At Nonna and Gramps's house, the night would be truly dark. The mountains stretched up and up into the clouds. It would be totally still and quiet.

Unless Star was howling, hemmed up in the deeper dark inside the barn. Calling for his pack.

Wanting to be let out, to run and hunt.

Chapter 22

Italy

'Shall we stop at the bridge for coffees and ice creams, as usual?' Nonna asked.

'Most definitely!' Gramps said. 'Pistachio and chocolate? Blackcurrant and cassis? What flavour for you today, Sylvie?'

'Vanilla with butterscotch, I think.'

Gramps parked the car, and Sylvie ran up the steep slope of the old stone bridge, to the top. The river rushed beneath, tumbling and frothing round the bridge supports, swollen with the melted snow from the mountains.

The signs of spring were all around.

'Look, Gramps! The swallows are here already!'
She watched the small birds swoop and dart over the
water, scooping up flies in their beaks as they flew.
They were building nests in the gaps between stones
under the arches of the bridge.

'Swallows won't arrive in England for another
month,' Gramps called back. 'Spring comes earlier here!'

Sylvie ran back down the bridge and crossed the
road with Nonna and Gramps to the café. She listened
to Gramps talking to the man at the counter. She was
proud of how well she understood Italian as well as
English. At the new school with Holly in September,
you could do Italian as one of your lessons. Perhaps
Holly could learn it too.

Sylvie took her ice cream outside to the table to
sit with Nonna. It was nice, just her being here. The
flight had been more fun by herself, too. The air host-
ess had given her a peppermint to suck for take-off
and another one for landing.

'Bella and Star will need a long walk when we get
back,' Nonna said, once they were back in the car for

the last leg of the journey. 'We left Star in the barn. We're being extra careful, now, because of Uncle Vince's concerns.'

'I think it's really sad for Star. And Uncle Vince is being horrible.'

'Finding a dead lamb is horrible too,' Nonna said. 'You have to understand: Vince is a farmer. Farming is a business. Losing a lamb costs him money.'

'How come Bella hasn't ever chased sheep?'

'Well, she's from a long line of sheep-herding dogs. It's in her genes, to round up and protect the flock, rather than chase and hunt. Very occasionally you get a dog that wants to chase and kill, but those get bred out.'

Sylvie thought about what she was saying. 'How come Star doesn't have that gene too? Or maybe he does. Uncle Vince doesn't have any proof it was Star who killed the lambs.'

Nonna and Gramps exchanged glances. Nonna turned round to face Sylvie.

'I'm afraid it doesn't look good. He's already killed two of the hens in our garden.'

Sylvie bit her lip to stop herself from crying. She was quiet for the rest of the journey.

Bella was excited to see her. She wagged her tail round and round in circles, and made soft, happy whimpering noises in her throat. When Sylvie sat down at the table under the vine, Bella laid her silky head on Sylvie's lap, and every time Sylvie stopped smoothing her ears and head, Bella lifted a front paw and nudged her to keep stroking.

'I'll take you out soon, Bella, I promise.' Sylvie kissed the top of her head. 'Now I need to see Star.'

Five hens were pecking at the grass in their run. Most of the grass was worn away; there were big bald patches of red-brown earth. It made Sylvie sad to see that: it didn't happen when the hens had the whole garden and the orchard to run and scratch about in.

Star was scraping at the barn door with his paws, his claws shredding the wood. Every so often he stopped, as if to listen, and then he barked and the barks turned to a kind of howl that made Sylvie feel slightly afraid. She knew it was wrong, keeping him imprisoned like that. No wonder he wanted to run and chase and kill things when he finally got free.

Gramps had come with her, carrying the old

leather lead. 'Open the door, Sylvie,' he said, 'and I'll catch hold of his collar.'

Star was quiet, listening to their voices. Sylvie lifted the iron latch and opened the door slowly. Star scrabbled at it, then pushed as it opened wider and he ran out, tail high and wagging, excited to see her. He jumped up, and Gramps grabbed his collar and clipped on the lead.

'He's grown!' Of course he had; but Sylvie couldn't stop herself saying it out loud. It was a shock to see how big he was now, with the fine long legs and big ears of the European wolf: *Canis Lupus Italicus.*

He pulled and bounced and jerked his head at the lead. 'Steady,' Gramps said firmly. 'Sit, Star.'

For a second, Star did actually sit.

'You've been training him, Gramps.'

'I've done my best, Sylvie, but without much success. He'll sit when it pleases him, and he'll come when it's food he's after, but he's a will of his own, this one. He's more wolf than anything, I reckon. He's nothing like his mother.'

'I'm sorry,' Sylvie said. 'It's all my fault, for wanting to keep him so much.'

Gramps reached out and gently touched her shoulder. 'No, you can't be thinking like that, Sylvie love. Nonna and I agreed we'd keep him, remember? What's done is done. But it breaks my heart to tie him up all the time. It's like keeping a wild animal in a cage. It's cruel, that's the truth of it.'

Sylvie shivered. The wind was blowing from the mountains. 'I'll get my coat and boots and I'll take Bella and Star for a walk, Gramps. By myself.'

Gramps looked unsure. 'He's strong, mind. He could pull you right over if he wanted to. But he's usually good enough, if Bella's there too. Keep him on the lead all the way, yes?'

'I know. Wait here for me? While I fetch my coat?'

Sylvie took the lead from Gramps's hand. She wound it tightly round her wrist. Star looked at her, his tongue lolling from his mouth which curved slightly as if he were smiling at her. She patted his head, and then ran her hand along the thick fur on his back. He leant against her legs, enjoying the attention. 'You be good, Star,' she whispered, and his ears pricked as if he were listening and understanding everything she said.

Bella fell into step beside them as they crossed the garden, out onto the track. Sylvie looked back once: Nonna and Gramps were standing at the door, watching her. She waved, turned again and carried on walking.

The two dogs trotted beside her.

Chapter 23

❧

Now that he was out in the open, Star seemed much more settled and calm. He walked between her and Bella, hardly pulling on the lead at all. Sylvie let it fall slack; she stopped whenever Star stopped to sniff the grass, or do a wee, letting him take as much time as he wanted. Smelling everything was how a dog made sense of his world, she knew that. And a wolf's sense of smell is hundreds of times more sensitive than a person's.

The field was dotted with the tiny flowers of early spring: a carpet of blue and white and yellow. Everything was coming back to life after the winter. Birds called; insects buzzed and hummed. Sylvie, Bella, and Star crossed the stream, high and bubbling under the wooden bridge, and took the ancient mule path up into the forest.

The trees were already coming into leaf: the sun lit up the newly unfurled leaves and bathed everything in a bright green light. The forest smelt new and fresh and delicious.

As they began the steep climb uphill, the stone track became too narrow for all three of them to walk side-by-side. Bella rushed ahead, which made Star pull and tug at the lead, as if he too wanted to be out at the front. It was hard to hold on to the lead now. Her hands hurt, the leather cutting into her palms. She panted, out of breath as she tried to keep up. 'Wait, Bella!' she called, and Bella did stop briefly as if to check Sylvie was following, but she didn't wait for long, and Star was still pulling on the lead, running and tugging her faster than she could manage.

All he wants is to catch up Bella, Sylvie thought. He needs to go at his own pace. We're so far up now, there's no way he's going to run back down to the farm and the lambing pastures. She yanked back the lead. 'Stay, Star! Just wait one second!'

Maybe the cross tone of her voice surprised him. He did stop, long enough for her to reach out and unclip the lead from his collar. Free, he bounded forwards again, running after Bella and then trotting quite calmly again beside her.

See! Sylvie imagined telling Gramps. *He's fine when he can go at his own pace. He just hates being tied up.*

In the dappled sunlight, Star merged into the forest ahead, almost invisible as he slipped between the tall trunks of the beeches and sweet chestnut trees. His grey and golden fur was perfect camouflage.

Now she too could walk freely, following behind the two dogs at her own pace. She began to relax. It was so much nicer walking like this. And Bella and Star were both happy.

She put her hand in her pocket to get out the little camera she'd borrowed from Mum. She wanted her own photos of Star, not just the ones that Nonna took for her. She stopped and took two of Bella and Star together, trotting between the trees. She pressed the button to make them look closer. She put the camera back in her coat pocket and hurried on to catch them up. The birds were quieter the deeper they went into the forest. Her footsteps seemed to ring out in the silence. Ahead, Bella barked and Star joined in with his *yip-yipping* sound: a higher note that seemed to echo out and spread through the trees, filling the space.

Sylvie kept climbing. This part of the forest was the deepest and darkest. Creepers hung from the trees. Ferns grew big and luscious in the shady damp places and the branches of the oldest trees were draped with the grey-green lichens that grow very, very slowly in places where the air is clean and pollution-free. The dogs were way ahead of her now. She felt like an animal herself, stepping quietly through this magical place.

The trees became more widely spaced again, and sunlight came through the gaps between them, letting grass and wild flowers grow underneath. Outcrops of white-grey rock pushed through the thin soil. She was almost through the forest, at the edge of the mountains.

'Bella? Star?' she called. Her voice bounced back at her off the rock. She needed to rest. She sat down on a wind-smoothed boulder. She could see Bella now, waiting for her, panting, her sides going in and out. And Star was just beyond her: standing on another outcrop of rock. He looks totally at home here, Sylvie thought. As if this is where he really belongs.

This side of the mountain was sheltered from the wind. Sylvie sat for a while, watching the pattern of shade and sun moving across the rock as clouds scudded across the sky. A bird of prey circled high above her, wings outstretched, riding the currents of air. Her eyes ached from the brightness of the light, so she closed them for a while, and lay back against the smooth curve of stone. Another few months and it would be summer, and so hot she would need to search for shade rather than lie out on the mountain like this. Holly might be coming with her for a holiday in July: they had talked with her mum and dad about it last night.

Only last night! It already seemed ages ago that she'd stayed over at Holly's. Another life. That was the thing about living in two places. It was like having two different lives. At some point, Sylvie thought, maybe you have to choose one of them, rather than always moving between the two, trying to balance them both.

Was that Star, yelping and yipping again in the distance? Sylvie sat up to look for him. But no, he was lying panting next to Bella, looking intently up to the top of the mountain ridge above them.

Sylvie looked too. She screwed her eyes up against the brightness, trying to see what Star could see.

Mountain goats, perhaps? She'd seen them before up here: a whole flock of brown and white chamois goats with their twisted horns and funny bearded faces. But goats didn't yelp.

Star sat bolt upright. Bella rolled over and sat up too, yawning. She growled softly in her throat, like a warning sound.

Star's ears were pricked, listening intently.

'It's all right, Star,' Sylvie said. 'Lie down. Good boy.'

Bella stayed sitting up, growling. The fur along her spine bristled.

Sylvie felt the hairs rise on the back of her own neck. There must definitely be something there, for Bella to growl like that.

As she watched, something moved out of the shadow of a rock. An animal, quite large, followed by another. Not a goat, or a sheep. They moved as one: three silvery-grey and golden wolves, stepping silently out onto the plateau of rock at one end of the high jagged ridge.

Sylvie held her breath. It was a miracle, to see real wild wolves at last, after all these years of looking and hoping. They were too far away for her to see them clearly. But she was sure that's what they were, now.

Bigger and slimmer with longer legs than a dog. And
that colouring, just like Star.

She looked at Star. He was standing up, now, his
nose and tail high, scenting the air. He whimpered,
took a few paces forwards.

'Stay, Star,' Sylvie said firmly. 'Lie down.'

Bella padded back towards Sylvie, sat down close
to her. They watched the wolves as they moved across
the ridge, silhouetted now against the bright blue sky.
Three wolves, a small pack. Just a family of juvenile
wolves, moving away from the main pack, perhaps,
Sylvie thought, remembering from her wolf book. She

reached out a hand to smooth Bella's fur. 'Good girl,' she said. 'It's all OK.'

But Star was moving forwards, further away from her and Bella. His whole body quivered with excitement. He lifted his head and yelped, and then the yelp changed and became the first part of a howl, and before Sylvie realized what was happening, he was running, and the wolves on the ridge had stopped to howl too, a thin, lonely cry that echoed across the mountain.

Sylvie scrambled up, her hand searching for the lead in her pocket. She ran after Star, calling his name.

But the ground was rocky and steep, and he went so much faster than she did. He jumped and ran, scrabbling up the steep mountain side, following the path the wild wolves had taken.

She stopped to watch. They'd disappeared over the ridge. And Star was still running, running, as fast as he could go, as if something irresistible was calling him, something he could not refuse.

The wolves were calling him home.

Sylvie watched, tears running down her cheeks. But deep inside, she knew that Star needed to go. That this was what he'd always needed. That he was too much of a wild animal ever to be happy with her.

She watched, and wept, until he had completely disappeared.

Chapter 24

S he knew he wouldn't come back. She waited for a
long time, just in case.

Bella grew restless. She whimpered, and fidgeted.
She sighed heavily and flumped down next to Sylvie,
resting her head on her paws. She looked at Sylvie with
her big brown eyes and whined. But she didn't seem to
mind that Star had gone. Perhaps that was the natural
way of things with a mother dog and a grown-up pup.

Finally Sylvie stood up. Her legs hurt from sitting still for so long. She stretched. The light was
changing, the sun much lower in the sky. 'Time to go
home,' she said.

Bella leapt up. She trotted across the grass towards the forest edge and the path down, wagging her tail as if she was relieved to be moving again. In her excitement she barked loudly, three times.

Sylvie turned so she could listen out one last time for an answering bark. For a moment she imagined Star coming back along the ridge, bounding down the slope towards them. But there wasn't a sound: only the whispering of the wind in the trees, and the far-off lonely cry of a buzzard.

She remembered what she'd read about the way a young stranger wolf would be let into a pack. How the animals would circle and sniff each other. The new wolf would probably take the submissive pose, tail between his legs, crouched down to show he was friendly and not a threat. Gradually, the others would accept him. They would start to lick and nuzzle his face. He would learn to hunt for rabbits and mice and eventually deer or even wild boar. Wolves hunt together, as a pack. They work and play and sleep together. They howl to call to each other, to stay connected. Star would be part of all that, eventually.

She thought about all this as she slowly walked back through the forest. He would be all right.

There would be plenty of food in the mountains in summer. He would have all the space he needed to run and roam, and he would have the companions he needed to play and fight and sleep with. Bit by bit, he would forget his puppyhood in the valley, and he would be his true wild self in the high Apennine mountains.

The only sign of what he'd been before would be his collar. Perhaps someone would spot him, one day: the wolf with the leather collar, like a dog.

'Sylvie! Thank goodness!'

Nonna and Gramps were walking up the mule path to meet her. Bella ran ahead to greet them.

Sylvie felt her face flush. She held the empty lead in one hand. They would see instantly that she had undone the lead and let Star go.

Tears came into her eyes. And Nonna saw and understood at once. Sylvie hardly needed to tell her what had happened.

'You were out so long! We were worried,' Gramps said. 'That's why we came looking for you.'

Nonna held her tight while she sobbed and told them everything. 'It's OK,' Nonna whispered into Sylvie's hair, over and over. 'It's how it was meant to be.'

Back at the house, Nonna ran Sylvie a deep bath. She brought her a thick new towel, warm from the kitchen, and a mug of hot chocolate.

'Later, we will go up to Vince and Maria's,' Nonna said. 'We'll tell them the story. You can talk to Mamma and Dad over Skype, and tell Holly, too, if you'd like to. And we'll remind Vince that the wolves are a protected species, here in Italy. We can talk to him about the Maremma. Don't worry about Star, Sylvie. He's going to be safe, and he will be happier, now.'

At bedtime, Sylvie lay in her bed with the shutters and the windows wide open. The night was still and starry; the wind had dropped. She listened and listened, long after Nonna and Gramps had gone to bed, and finally it came, the sound she was waiting for.

Very far away, from the remote mountains, came the sound of wolves, howling.

Sylvie liked to think it was three wolves, and one wolf-dog.

Star, saying goodbye.

Epilogue

❦

'He's here!' Mum called from the kitchen.

Sylvie and Holly rushed to the front window of the flat. A green van was parking in front of the bookshop on the double yellow lines. The writing on the side read: Richard Wood Fresh Veg Boxes and Free-range Eggs.

'Come on!' Sylvie tugged Holly behind her. They clattered down the stairs and out onto the street. Mum followed behind.

A young man with a shaved head and muddy boots was lifting a cardboard box out of the back of the van. 'Hello!' he said. 'Want to take a first peek at them?'

Sylvie nodded. He opened the top of the box just a little, enough for her to see six beady eyes, a glimpse of brown feathers. She smiled.

'Three young 'uns, as ordered,' the man said. 'Now, where are we taking them?'

Sylvie and Holly led the way through to the door into the back garden. Without the tatty old shed it looked much bigger. Instead of the concrete paving there was a square of real grass lawn, pots of red and pink geraniums, a vine beginning to grow up against the white-painted wall, a table and chairs. In the other half of the garden stood a wooden hen house with a wire run.

The man put the box down. 'You're in charge, your mum tells me,' he said to Sylvie. 'All yours.'

Sylvie lifted the first hen out of the box. She held it firmly, close to her for a second. The hen's feathers were warm and soft; Sylvie felt its heart beating fast against her hand. 'It's OK, sweetie,' she whispered. She let the hen free in the run and went back for the next. 'Do you want a go?' she asked Holly.

Holly shook her head. 'You do it. You know how to hold them properly.'

There were two reddish-brown hens and one smaller, white one. The three hens shook themselves, and twitched their feathers. They explored the run and walked up the ramp into their house. Sylvie heard them rustling the hay in the nesting box. They came back down the ramp, pecked at the food hopper and scratched the grass. The little white hen had a drink from the shiny new water trough. Sylvie noticed a little patch of silver-grey feathers on its head, like a star.

'Perfect,' the man said. 'They'll be very happy with you, I can tell. They won't start laying eggs for a few more weeks, though.'

'I know that!' Sylvie said.

The man laughed. 'Well, I'll be off now.'

Mum went with the man back to the van.

Sylvie and Holly settled down to watch the hens some more.

'They're funny and sweet,' Holly said. 'They make a lovely sound, don't they?'

Sylvie watched the little white hen peck at a caterpillar it had found. It made a crooning sound in its throat. The hens made her think of Italy, and Nonna and Gramps, and so many happy times in their garden. Hens were nothing like a dog, but they were lovely in their own particular way.

'We need to think of names, next,' Sylvie said. 'And then I'm going to take a photo of them and email it to Nonna and Gramps.'

At bedtime, after Sylvie had shut the hens up safely in their house for the night, she stayed a little longer in the garden. Even with all the bright city lights reflecting up into the sky, she could see one star, and then another . . . and she knew the moon would rise soon, casting its mysterious silver shadows over the city, over the park and the trees and shops and offices and schools and Holly's garden.

The same moon would be rising over Nonna and Gramps' house, too, over the garden. Bella would yawn and stretch out on her blue blanket, her paws touched with silver.

Up in the Apennine mountains, perhaps Star would be running along a high ridge, and the moonlight would catch his fur and turn it silver too. Maybe he would remember, like a dim shadow, his time as a puppy with Sylvie. Perhaps he would stop, and look up at the rising moon. And then he would run on silently on his silver-tipped paws, wild and free.

By the author of
Sylvie and Star

Turn the page for
chapter one

Chapter 1

ᕼ

Something was different.

The fox sensed it.

Curled up in its daytime hiding place in a nest of brambles, the fox lifted its head. It pricked up both ears to listen.

It heard a car, and voices. Next, a big removal lorry drew up on the road outside the house. Someone banged a door at the back as they opened it.

For hours, the removal men went to and fro, carrying boxes into the house. Tables and chairs came next; beds and bookcases, lamps and cushions and rugs. A whole house-load of things was carried out of the lorry, up the front path, through the open door into the house.

All day, the fox tried to sleep, curled round with the tip of its tail wrapped round its body, but its ears twitched, listening out for danger.

As evening came and shadows lengthened across the grass, the lorry drove away. The front door banged shut. At last it was quiet—just the normal sounds of an autumn evening. A blackbird sang at the top of a tree. A squirrel ran along the edge of the rickety wooden fence.

The fox uncurled itself. It yawned, and stretched.

Silently, on velvet paws, it slipped through the bars of the gate into the garden. No one saw its slim, red-brown body and long tail as it stopped at the edge of the lawn to sniff the night air. It looked up at the house.

The fox called out, into the dark. It was a strange sound, an eerie, high-pitched scream that echoed round the night garden and made everything afraid.

JULIA GREEN is the author of more than ten novels for children and teenagers, and this is her second book for Oxford University Press. As a child, Julia lived in a village called Ashtead, in Surrey. She did a degree in English at the University of Kent and an MPhil in English Studies at Oxford University. Julia lives in Bath and is Course Director for the MA in Writing for Young People at Bath Spa University. She has two sons. You can find out more about Julia by going to her website at **www.julia-green.co.uk**

More Oxford books you might enjoy ...

Something lives deep within the forest . . .
something that has not been seen on
Callum's farm for over a hundred years.

Callum and Iona make a promise
to keep their amazing discovery secret,
but can they keep it safe from harm?

The pact they make will change lives forever.

ISBN 978-0-19-275624-4

'The white dolphin is a sign that Mum's out there . . . '

When they first meet, Kara and Felix can't stand each other.
But on discovering an injured dolphin calf on the beach they
know they must work together to save it.

Now friends, they set out to discover the truth behind the
disappearance of Kara's mother, and to protect the nearby reef.

But powerful people don't want them to succeed.
And with the odds stacked against them, how can Kara
and Felix make their voices heard?

ISBN 978-0-19-275621-3